LA CASA GRANDE

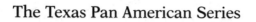
The Texas Pan American Series

Alvaro Cepeda Samudio

La Casa Grande

Translated by Seymour Menton
Foreword by Gabriel García Márquez

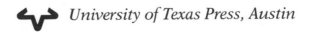 *University of Texas Press, Austin*

First edition, 1991

Requests for permission to reproduce material from this work
should be sent to Permissions, University of Texas Press,
Box 7819, Austin, TX 78713-7819.

∞ The paper used in this publication meets the minimum requirements
of American National Standard for Information Sciences—Permanence
of Paper for Printed Library Materials, ANSI Z39.48–1984.

Library of Congress Cataloging-in-Publication Data

Cepeda Samudio, Alvaro.
    [Casa grande. English]
    La casa grande / Alvaro Cepeda Samudio ; translated by Seymour
Menton; foreword by Gabriel García Márquez. — 1st ed.
    p. cm.
    ISBN 0-292-74667-9. — ISBN 0-292-74673-3 (pbk.)
    I. Title.
PQ8180.13.E6C313   1991
863—dc20
                        90-45639
                           CIP

The Texas Pan American Series is published with the assistance of a
revolving publication fund established by the Pan American Sulphur
Company.

For Alejandro Obregón

CONTENTS

Plaque on the front of La Casa Grande in the city of Ciénaga: "The action of *La casa grande*, a novel written by Alvaro Cepeda Samudio (1926–1972), beloved son of Ciénaga, takes place in this house, which belonged to General Francisco de Labarces Perea, head of the Radicalist Movement."

Front view of La Casa Grande in Ciénaga, where the action of the novel takes place.

INTRODUCTION   « ix »

In the last chapter of García Márquez's *One Hundred Years of Solitude*, Aureliano Babilonia's four friends leave Macondo. Alfonso (Fuenmayor) and Germán (Vargas) planned to return, "but nothing more was ever heard of them" (Avon Books, 1971, p. 371). Gabriel (García Márquez) "left for Paris with two changes of clothing, a pair of shoes, and the complete works of Rabelais" (p. 371). Alvaro (Cepeda Samudio), the author of *La casa grande* (1962), "bought an eternal ticket on a train that never stopped traveling" (p. 370). The train goes through Louisiana, Kentucky, Arizona, and Michigan and is a fictionalized version of Cepeda Samudio's trip to the United States for the main purpose of studying journalism at Columbia University. When he rejoined his friends in Barranquilla, he reinforced their efforts to liberate Colombian fiction from the *costumbrista* and academic traditions of the highland departments of Antioquia, Caldas, and Cundinamarca.

Cepeda Samudio was born in Ciénaga in 1926 and may have witnessed, at the age of two, the famous massacre of the striking banana workers in the railroad station. He attended elementary school and high school at the English-language Colegio Americano in Barranquilla. A professional journalist like García Márquez, Cepeda Samudio began his career with *El Nacional* in August 1947. In April 1950, the four friends founded the literary-sports weekly *Crónica* and for eight months published a foreign short story in each issue. Cepeda Samudio continued to push for a renovation of Colombian prose fiction in his column "Brújula de la cultura" ("Cultural Compass") in *El Heraldo* of Barranquilla. In September 1951 he praised Julio Cortázar's first volume of short stories, *Bestiario*, only five months after it was published in Buenos Aires.

Cepeda was also the Colombian representative for the St. Louis–based *Sporting News* and later became editor-in-chief of the *Diario del Caribe*.

The publication in 1954 of Cepeda's first volume of short stories, *Todos estábamos a la espera* ("Everyone Was Waiting"), created quite a stir in Colombian literary circles. Directly inspired by Hemingway, the lead story is narrated in the first person by the protagonist without any intervention by the traditional moralizing and artistic omniscient narrator. The open ending is in keeping with the process of forcing the reader to collaborate actively in the story.

«*x*»

Whereas Hemingway was the model for Cepeda's short stories, his more famous novel, *La casa grande* ("The Big House") was directly inspired by Faulkner, and particularly by *The Sound and the Fury*. Temporal and spatial planes change abruptly; the participants in dialogues are not identified by name; characters are referred to by pronoun or by generic names such as Father, Mother, Sister, Brother involving three generations of the same family; family relationships are complicated by the suggestion of father-daughter and sibling incest; and the same events are presented from many different points of view. Nevertheless, *La casa grande* is an authentically Colombian novel that intertwines the tragic story of a family dominated by a tyrannical father and subsequently by his eldest daughter with the 1928 massacre. As such, along with Héctor Rojas Herazo's *Respirando el verano* ("Gasping for Breath") (1962), *La casa grande* is one of the important forerunners of *One Hundred Years of Solitude* and a spate of other novels published in the 1960s, 1970s, and 1980s by authors from Colombia's Atlantic Coast. Cepeda's second collection of stories, *Los cuentos de Juana*, was published in Barranquilla in 1972, the year he died in New York.

*   *   *

I am extremely grateful to Germán Vargas for having suggested this translation project to me and for having helped in obtaining the authorization from the family of Cepeda Samudio; and to Roberto Herrera Soto for the illustrations and for having helped in the translation of some of the regional words and phrases.

Gabriel García Márquez 1967

FOREWORD

La casa grande is a novel based on a historical event: the 1928 banana workers' strike on the Atlantic Coast of Colombia which was settled by army bullets. Its author, Alvaro Cepeda Samudio, at the time only two years old, was living in a large wooden house with six windows and a balcony full of dusty potted flowers opposite the railroad station where the massacre took place. Nevertheless, in this book, there is not a single person killed and the only soldier who remembers having plunged his bayonet into a man in the darkness doesn't have his uniform splattered with blood "but with shit."

This manner of writing history, arbitrary as it may seem to the historians, is a splendid lesson in poetic transformation. Without distorting reality or playing loose with the serious political and human aspects of the social drama, Cepeda Samudio has subjected it to a kind of purifying alchemy and has given us only its mythical essence, which will remain forever, far longer than man's morality, justice, and ephemeral memory. The superb dialogues, the straightforward and virile richness of the language, the genuine compassion aroused by the characters' fate, the fragmentary and somewhat loose structure which so closely resembles the pattern of memories—everything in this book is a magnificent example of how a writer can honestly filter out the immense quantity of rhetorical and demagogic garbage that stands in the way of indignation and nostalgia.

For this reason, *La casa grande*, besides being a beautiful novel, is a risky experiment, and an invitation to meditate on the unforeseen, arbitrary, and astounding techniques of poetic creation. And for this same reason, it represents a new and formidable contribution to the most important literary phenomenon in today's world: the Latin American novel.

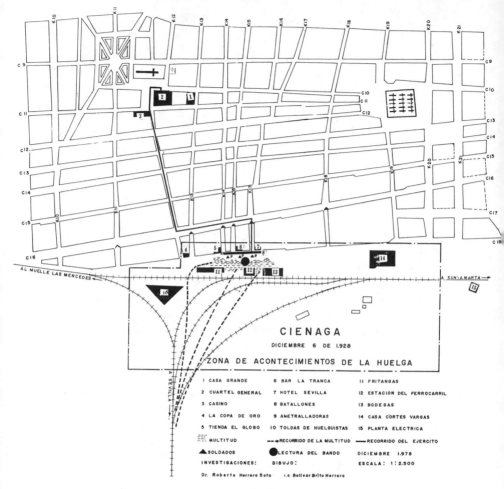

Street map of Ciénaga, site of the events related to the strike, December 6, 1928, prepared by Dr. Roberto Herrera Soto. Key places mentioned in this novel and *One Hundred Years of Solitude* are: (1) the Big House; (2) the Barracks; (4) the bar La Copa de Oro or (6) the bar La Tranca or (7) Hotel Sevilla; (8) the batallions; (9) the machine guns; (11) food stands; (12) railroad station; (14) the house of General Carlos Cortés Vargas.

● Spot where the edict was read ordering the strikers to disperse.

▤ Where the strikers had gathered

▲ Soldiers posted at corners to block access to the railroad station.

THE SOLDIERS

—Are you awake?

—Yeah.

—I haven't been able to sleep either: the rain drenched my blanket.

—How come it's raining so much if it's the wrong time of year? Why do you think it's raining so much?

—Don't know. It is the wrong time of year.

—Do you want a cigarette?

—All right.

—Damn it: they're all soaked.

—It doesn't matter.

—How are we going to smoke them like that?

—It doesn't matter.

—Nothing ever matters to you. I'll bet it doesn't even matter to you that the rain hasn't let us sleep.

—The rain doesn't bother me.

—Then why haven't you slept?

—I've been thinking.

—About what?

—About tomorrow.

—Are you afraid? The lieutenant said they're armed, but I don't think so.

—I've been thinking about why they sent us.

—Didn't you hear what the lieutenant said: they don't want to work, they left the plantations and they're looting the towns.

—It's a strike.

—Yeah, but they don't have the right. They also want their wages raised.

—They're on strike.

—Of course: and that's why they've sent us here: to put down the strike.

—That's what I don't like. That's not our job.

—What's not our job?

—To put down strikes.

—Our job is everything. I'm glad I came. I've never been in the Zone. And to be on active duty is better than to be in the barracks: you don't have to line up for inspection, they don't call on you for reports about your assignments, and they can't put you in the guardhouse.

—They sure can.

« 4 » —How can they if we're on active duty?

—I don't know, but they sure can.

—Just the same it's better than being in the barracks.

—Yeah, but it's not right.

—What does it matter if it's right or not. What's important is that we're on active duty and not in the barracks.

—It does matter.

—Now it matters; the problem is that you're afraid.

—I'm not a bit afraid.

—Then why are you worried?

—Because if it's a strike, we have to respect it and not get involved.

—They're the ones who have to show respect.

—To whom?

—To the authorities, to us.

—We're not the authorities: we're soldiers: the police are the authorities.

—O.K., but the police are no good. That's why they sent for us.

—What's happening is that the police haven't been able to cope with them.

—You're afraid.

—Bull. I'm not afraid; the thing is I don't like the idea of putting down a strike. Who knows? Maybe the strikers are the ones who are right.

—They have no right.

—Right to do what?

—To strike.

—A lot you know.

—The lieutenant said so.

—The lieutenant doesn't know anything.

—Well, that's true.

—He repeats what the major says.

—This morning, when we were tying up our knapsacks, he said: only the lightweight blankets and the straw mats. And then when we were about to board the ship, he made us undo our knapsacks, take out the lightweight blankets and straw mats, and sent us to the store for the heavy blankets. They've decided to send you on the barges instead of on the sheltered deck, he said. He doesn't know a damn thing.

—Who said they were armed?

« 5 »

—The lieutenant, when they lined us up for briefing. Didn't you hear?

—No.

—Where do you think they got their arms from?

—They don't have any arms: only machetes.

—How do you know?

—They're day laborers.

—And that's why they can't have arms?

—Yeah, that's why.

—Help me wring out the blanket because when we enter the channels, the mosquitoes will come out. Grab the other end. Where's your blanket? Didn't you cover yourself with your blanket?

—No.

—You got soaked through and through.

—So what.

—What did you do with your blanket?

—I wrapped my rifle in it so that it wouldn't get wet.

*   *   *

They had made them march from the barracks to the harbor that afternoon. The distance was short, but their boots were new and too big and the new leather of the cartridge belts and knapsacks had not yet been broken in by their sweat.

In the harbor, they made them wait several hours. There were many of them and the lifeboats had to be secured before they could go on board. The boarding went slowly. They had to do it through the stern of the ship and the nails on their boots were continually slipping on the smooth boards. While they were waiting, they had been ordered to put their guns in their bandoliers, but the barrels collided with the low cross-beams and since they couldn't squeeze through the passage-ways on either side of the boiler with their canteens and knap-sacks strapped on, they had to take them off and move through the ship to where the lifeboats were with their equipment in their hands. The boarding was slow and full of confusion. When the last soldiers' turn finally came, they had been wait-ing for several hours. They accommodated themselves in the « 6 »   lifeboats with their rifles between their knees.

Some became frightened during the crossing of the river: there was a strong December wind, and the lifeboats moved forward clumsily, out of synch with the ships, which were al-ternately tightening and extending the cables as they neatly ground the wooden splinters against the gunwales. Those who were in the bows of the ships got wet.

Before entering the channel, they could see the whole city lit up on the other side. They had never seen it before.

Each one thought he could recognize the light of familiar places. The initial surprise caused them to form groups: friends looked for each other above other heads that were stretching in search of their friends. Each one said: there's the barracks: and they pointed with their arms in every direction.

They entered the channel as if it were a tunnel. The overly wide lifeboats and the ships with their overly long barges, ran up against the mangrove-lined banks hurling them on top of one another, with the soldiers having to dodge constantly in order to keep from being hit by the vertically held rifles.

Everything that was new: the incredible stream of fire from the smokestacks, the clumsy movements of the ships obeying with precision the bell's unpredictable sounds, the banks that would suddenly open up revealing a hut, a small fire, and a dog's barking: everything that was new became familiar, repe-titious, monotonous. Then sleep began to double them over on their rifles, against the stowage battens, against each other's shoulders, backs, and sides.

Suddenly and unexpectedly, it began to rain.

*　　　*　　　*

—I'm hungry. Have we arrived yet?

—Yeah.

—A long time ago?

—No. Just now.

—I fell asleep as soon as we entered the channels. I didn't feel anything. Did you sleep?

—No.

—Lots of mosquitoes in the channel?

—No.

—It's a lie that there'd be waves of mosquitoes in the chan- « 7 » nels. I knew it was a lie.

—It wasn't a lie.

—Did it keep on raining the whole night?

—Yeah.

—Why are we stopped here?

—They're lowering the lifeboat.

—Where are we going to have our coffee? I'm hungry.

—I don't know; maybe in the station.

—Why in the station? You don't mean to tell me that there aren't any barracks here. Besides we have to put our blankets out to dry if the sun decides to come out today. You have to dry your khakis.

—I doubt that they'll give us time to dry anything.

—Did the others land yet?

—No, we're the first.

—Get up: they've started to leave the ship. I'm stiff. Damn rain.

—We've still got time to get off.

—But the guys up front are getting off. We ought to wait until it gets light: you can't see a thing.

—They're in a hurry.

—What for? Ah, to put an end to the strike.

—Perhaps we can't put an end to the strike.

—Of course we can put an end to it.

—Perhaps not.

—Then you too think they're armed.

—No, they're not armed.

—This damn thing is going to be easy.

—Who knows.

—Get up, now it's our turn to get off.

—You're in a hurry too.

—No, I don't care what the hell happens to the strike. I'm stiff and I'm hungry.

—Move ahead then.

—No, wait: I'm going to piss here so I can leave this place really soaked.

*   *   *

« 8 »

When the boats bumped against the soggy banks and came to rest, those who were asleep began to wake up. It was not yet dawn. They woke up slowly: first their arms and legs and bodies recalled the proximity of other arms, other legs, and other bodies: then their hands let go of the rifles and grabbed them again in order to recognize their shape and weight: finally their eyes began to make out points of reference in the darkness.

The ship's searchlights carefully scanned the tops of the boats. Almost like an insult. The light smacked them in the eyes like an open, burning slap. Some protected their faces with their free arms; others barely turned around and the light slid down their caps and their wet necks. Now they were all awake.

The landing was less slow and less confusing. They were eager to move about and to arrive. They didn't care that they had to throw themselves into the thick water that separated the boats' prows from the shore. They wanted to move about. They threw themselves in the water and the bottom gave way under the double weight of the bodies and the equipment. Their legs sank into the mud splashing up a stench. But they disembarked quickly and almost speedily crossed the space that separated them from the shore and scrambled up the embankment using their rifle butts for leverage.

*   *   *

—The only thing that was dry were my boots: now I'm completely soaked. I'm going to take them off.

—We still have to walk to the station.

—Just to empty them: they're full of water.

—The station is far away.

—Very far?

—About a league.

—And where the hell are we going to get some coffee?

—In the station.

—We should camp here and have some coffee and then we can go wherever they want us to.

—We have to be in the station when the train arrives.   « 9 »

—The train? What train?

—The one that's going to take us to the Zone.

—That's right. Now I know. You explained it to me last night but I had forgotten: hungry as I am, it's hard to keep up with anything. What time does the train leave?

—I don't think it has a fixed time today. The employees are on strike.

—They too? And what do they have to do with the farm laborers?

—Nothing.

—Then they're sticking their noses into somebody else's business.

—No. They don't have any job security either. They stopped running the trains in order to help the strikers.

—Who's going to drive the train then?

—I don't know. They'll send a platoon to look for them and they'll force them to work.

—That's the way to do it.

—Why?

—Because otherwise how are we going to get to the towns to put down the strike?

—It would be better if we couldn't get to the towns. It would be better if we didn't have to kill anyone.

—What's better is not being in the barracks, like now. Look how soft my boots got with the water; I can hardly feel them. What's bad is that when the sun heats up, they'll become hard as rocks again.

—The engineers ought to hide.

—What?

—Nothing.

—Feel this boot: you see how soft it is. Wet yours so that they'll soften up too.

—They are wet.

—Take them off and dry them as I did: you stick them in the water and take them out; stick them in and take them out; stick them in and take them out; they get soft and clean. Do it and you'll see.

—There's no time: here comes the sergeant giving the order
« 10 » to fall in.

—Why do we have to fall in?

—So that they can call the roll.

—What? Are they afraid that some recruit has fallen in the water? They shouldn't have sent recruits.

—No, not that they've fallen in the water but that they've flown the coop.

—Flown the coop? Why should they fly the coop when they're outside the barracks? It doesn't make sense; someone flies the coop when he's inside.

—I'm telling you that someone has deserted.

—A deserter, you mean that there may be a deserter.

—Yeah, if that's the way you want to put it.

—But there can't be a deserter when we're on a mission. There can only be a deserter when there's a war and we're not at war now; we're on a mission.

—All right then, he's fled; he's fled because he didn't want to take part in this.

—One hundred eighty-four.

—One hundred eighty-five.

*   *   *

—Do you want more coffee?

—I'm not hungry.

—After making us wait so long, all they give us is coffee. I'm still hungry.

—Take mine.

—Seriously, you don't want it?

—No. Give me a cigarette.

—They're not dry yet.

—I don't care; give it to me the way it is.

—How can you enjoy chewing it?

—It distracts me.

—Nothing distracts my guts. They're growling from hunger. Does chewing tobacco make your hunger go away?

—Yeah.

—I'm going to chew a little to see if it works. Where did you learn that?

—A long time ago, in my home town.

—So as not to feel hungry also? « 11 »

—Yeah. There was never enough food.

—Just like in the barracks.

—Here there's not enough food because the sergeants steal the money. At home it was because there wasn't any money.

—They steal the money and the food: I've bought food from the fellow in charge of distributing it and they say that the sergeant's wife has a store to sell what's removed from the warehouse.

—Whoever ordered this coffee must have pocketed a pretty penny: they didn't even provide a roll.

—I'm going to ask the women who brought the pots.

—What for? If the sergeant finds out you've been inquiring, he'll put you in the guardhouse.

—He can't put me in the guardhouse here; we're not in the barracks.

—He'll punish you some other way then.

—They ought to tell the major.

—The major also steals.

—I don't believe it.

—He's the one who steals the most.

—O.K., they all steal. But the sergeant is the worst because he steals from us: he steals our food money and makes us go hungry. If the major steals, he probably steals from the government and that doesn't matter.

—It matters more because he's stealing from the nation.

—The nation isn't the government; the nation is the flag. Stealing from the government isn't stealing, everyone knows that. Let's walk up to where those other guys are. O.K.?

—No, I have to clean my rifle; it got full of mud when we landed.

—Mine also got stuck in the mud, but I'm not going to clean it now.

—I am; I'm not going to walk around with a rusty rifle.

—You know what? There are women in this town.

—Who told you?

—Nobody. I saw them.

—Where?

—In that house on the corner, opposite the one that says hotel. I went to look for the women who made the coffee to see

if there was something else to eat; and the window was open; and I saw the women.

—Maybe they're not what you think.

—Yes they are: they have long dresses and their faces are all made up. Besides the parlor is decorated with crepe paper, like for a dance. Of course they are. Do you think we'll have time to drop by?

—I don't know.

—The only thing is that they don't seem French; they seem to be from here.

—Then they're not what you think.

* * *

—That train is never going to come.

—Better if it didn't.

—Why?

—Because then we wouldn't have to go.

—And if they make us march? It's better if it does come.

—They won't make us march.

—How do you know?

—The towns are pretty far away.

—Have you been in the towns?

—No.

—What town are we going to?

—I don't know. Probably to all of them.

—Are they all on strike?

—The Zone is on strike.

—And the Zone includes all the towns?

—Yeah.

—How many towns are there?

—I don't know.

—A lot?

—Yeah, a lot. You sure can ask questions.

—Don't you like it when I ask you questions?

—I don't care.

—I wish there were a lot of towns; in that way we'd take longer to put the strike down and we wouldn't have to return to the barracks. I'm getting bored waiting here; why doesn't that train come?

« 13 »

—They may not have found the engineers. Maybe they haven't been able to force them to come.

—We would have brought them by using our rifle butts. They must have sent some dumb jerks. We would have brought them a while ago.

—That's what you think.

—Damn right; I would have brought them by using my rifle butt. I don't think they're armed.

—You don't have any right to hit them. You can't force them to come if they don't want to.

—Of course we've got a right; that's why we're here.

—They're on strike.

—I know, but that doesn't matter.

—It sure does matter.

—O.K. Damn, why doesn't that train come?

*   *   *

—Do you think they'll give us time to drop by to see the women?

—I don't know. I don't think so.

—What if the train doesn't come? They have to take us somewhere; we're not going to spend the whole day here in the station.

—If the train doesn't come today, they'll make us spend the night in the barracks.

—There are barracks in this town?

—Yeah.

—But there aren't any soldiers.

—Very few.
—Where are the barracks?
—In the square, across from the church.
—Have you been in this town before?
—No.
—Then how do you know?
—The barracks and the churches are always together, they're always in the squares.
—If we spend the night here, I'm taking off; I feel like dropping by that house with the women.

« 1 4 »

*   *   *

—I've never ridden on a train, have you?
—Yeah.
—Many times?
—Yeah.
—Do you like to ride on the train?
—I prefer to watch it go by.
—I've watched them go by but I've never gotten on.
—We lived for a while near a stop.
—Like this one?
—No, this is a station. There, it didn't always stop, only when there were passengers. We used to go every day to sell figs. When it didn't stop, we'd eat the figs ourselves at night.
—Then it was better when it didn't stop.
—No, because when it did stop we could sell some figs, and then we knew we'd be able to drink coffee for two or three mornings.
—I like figs better than coffee, don't you?
—I don't know; I haven't eaten figs for so long and there were so many mornings that we didn't have coffee that I've forgotten the difference.
—What were the figs like?
—Large and purple and full of seeds on the inside.
—What were the trains like?
—Long and lively; and when they didn't stop, the people used to wave to us; that was the best of all.
—The only train that I've seen is the one in Puerto Colom-

bia, but it's small and I haven't seen it run. When it's stopped, the people don't wave, do they?

—No, they don't wave; they just stare.

—This town is ugly.

—All towns are the same.

—But this one is uglier. I had never seen walls covered with salt. They don't have to buy salt here; all they have to do is scratch it off the walls.

—They don't eat that salt.

—Why not?

—I don't know, but they don't eat it.

« 15 »

—In these barracks, they don't make you work; everything is rusty and full of salt.

—Yeah, you're right.

—Did you notice that when we went by, nobody looked out? Not even the kids.

—That's because they know why we're here; they're angry at us already.

—Why should they be angry at us: it's not our fault.

—Who knows.

—It's the fault of the strikers.

—Of the strikers, no; of the Company.

—O.K., but not ours.

—Who knows.

—Did you see the house next door? It's big and extends to the other street: that's how we can escape tonight. And it's all closed up; do you think there are people in it?

—Sure there are.

—Never mind: the patio faces the barracks patio and the wall is low; that's how we can escape.

—Not me, I'm not in the mood.

—I am, I'm getting out tonight.

   *   *   *

From the station to the town barracks they walked. With their guns in their bandoliers and their knapsacks over their right shoulders, they walked on streets covered with hot salty mud and with puddles full of salt water and fresh water. Some of them took off their boots which had already dried off and splashed through the middle of the thick puddles. They walked slowly, in no hurry, looking at the closed doors and windows on both sides of the streets without comprehending.

They had spent the whole day in the station: the first ones sitting on the long wooden benches, the others strewn on the floor, leaning against the gray iron posts, squatting along the whole length of the platform. Some had slept, others had stared for a long time at the empty tracks which gradually came together as they faded into the distance lost in a fuzzy spot at the base of the mountain. They all became annoyed. They got tired of looking at the sealed shut town, the dead town that began across the street from the station. After a few hours they didn't care anymore; they gathered around what was familiar to them: their guns and knapsacks and their friends: and they no longer expected anything.

The distance between the station and the barracks was short and they walked it in silence, along silent streets past silent houses.

The barracks were dirty and almost unoccupied. They walked in as far as the central patio surrounded by arches and doors, paved with fresh red bricks. They began to fall in, dropping their knapsacks on one side and resting their guns on the other; they moved forward and backward, with short, continuous steps, lining up; then quietly, discreetly, they called off their numbers. By the time the order was given to break ranks, they knew what doors to head for and which cots they should toss their helmets on and spread out their blankets on. Now they were themselves once again: they had recovered their routine.

*　　*　　*

—Aren't you going to sleep?
—I'm not sleepy.
—Then you'll go with me.
—No.
—Do you have money?
—Yeah, two pesos.

—Will you lend me one?

—O.K.

—Are you sure you don't want to? Let's take off; they just sounded the call for silence.

—I'm not in the mood.

—Wait till you get a look at them; I tell you they don't look like whores.

—Maybe they aren't.

—Yes they are. I saw them. Let's go, maybe these are the kind that will let us take our pants off.

« 17 »

—I don't want to, I don't want to, do you hear me?

—O.K., don't get angry.

—I'm not angry, it's just that I don't want to go.

—I'll be right back. O.K.?

—Yeah.

—Are you going to stay awake again all night long?

—No. I'm going to sleep now.

—Keep an eye on my stuff, will you.

—Yeah. Be careful, they may be patrolling.

—Don't worry, they won't catch me. I wish we were going together.

—I'm not in the mood. If you're going to take off, get going now.

—I'll be right back.

—O.K.

*   *   *

The train was long and messy. Instead of being lively as all trains are, it was slow and clumsy, with the cars exposed to the rain, bumping into each other unnecessarily. The locomotive stopped opposite the station: the locomotive, not the last cars. The men riding in the engineer's cabin and on the roof of the second car didn't get off. They remained seated with their rifles between their legs, looking at the engineers.

When they gave the order to fall in, the men who were scattered throughout the train rushed forward and crowded together in front of the locomotive, as they had practiced. The group gradually assumed the form of a straight line, stretching, shrinking, until it became compact and uniform. When the noise of boots, rifles, and knapsacks subsided, they began to count off; there were very few of them. The first one turned to the right, raised his rifle, and began to walk; he crossed the station and entered the town. The others followed him with the same movement. The last two turned to the left, rested their guns horizontally on their cartridge belts, and began patrolling the platform up and down.

Then the whistle sounded short, sharp, cold: like a knife: like a signal.

« 18 »

The column stopped, piling up momentarily. Some turned their heads around, mechanically, without curiosity, without surprise, mechanically. Then, without comprehending, they continued walking.

*   *   *

The bugler on guard duty ran across the still-dark patio and got up on the bench. The clear, precise, familiar sound filled the whole barracks.

In the long, silent rooms, the rusty iron of the beds began to squeak, and for a moment, the sound of bodies, boots, canteens, guns, and above all the less precise sound of the rushing around drowned out the sound of the bugle.

They lined up four deep, with their backs to the bench, where they could still hear the bugle's urgent sound. Then the bugle fell silent and the large space where all the various sounds had been heard was slowly filled with the daylight that was beginning to fall on the patio.

They did not sound off by the numbers.

With precise steps, keeping in time to the voice that called the cadence, in line, with their guns slung over their shoulders and their knapsacks resting on their backs, they left the barracks. They marched through the same streets with each man's eyes fixed on the back of the man who marched in front of him, without looking sideways at the gaping holes of the open doors and windows. With firm steps, they marched through the puddles and the salty mud. The water in the puddles splashed up under the weight of their bodies: the double weight of metal and leather. The mud splattered brightly with the impact from each boot. They all marched up to the station in columns of four with only one column of three.

* * *

 They had not yet become death: but they were now carrying death on their fingertips: they were marching with death stuck to their legs: death was hitting their butts with every stride; death was weighing heavily on their left collarbones: a death made of metal and wood that they had carefully   « 19 » cleaned.

* * *

 Those who had stayed at the station gathered on the other side of the street, opposite the hotel. At first they were afraid; there were seven of them, but the men did not appear hostile and then all that remained was curiosity. They were there, on the other side of the street, still holding their rifles horizontally on their cartridge belts, simply looking, without understanding much of what was happening, without even trying to understand, only watching how the men were gradually arriving in groups emerging from all the streets and all the houses that had seemed deserted and empty. And when the groups came together at the station and were now a crowd, they boarded the coaches, the locomotive. And when there was no longer room in the coaches, they climbed up on top of the coaches and the locomotive. They took over the train, filling it with their clean clothes, their short-brimmed, yellow straw hats, and their machetes resting quietly within their constantly fingered sheaths. They covered the train, squeezing into the open cars and climbing on top of the closed cars, hanging from the brakemen's ladders and from the locomotive's steps. And they stayed on the train silent, determined, and peaceful.

* * *

 —I looked for you everywhere and couldn't find you. I was scared, I was scared when I heard so many shots. Why did they kill them: they didn't have any arms. You were right: they didn't have any arms. And now what are we going to do? I must go back, I want to see her by daylight, I want to see how she looks by daylight. Do you think we'll go back to the barracks? They're not going to let us stay here with all these corpses. You know, I didn't go to the whorehouse. I didn't have to. In the house next door, you remember, the one that was closed up, there are people. She must live there because she was in the patio, alone in the patio. I didn't see her face clearly. She didn't speak either. Then, a little while later, she began to cry, not shouting but softly: you almost couldn't hear that she was crying. I don't understand, I don't understand anything. You must go back with me, you must explain it to me. She didn't touch me, she didn't even grab on to me, she didn't even raise her arms. With her eyes open she let herself. I didn't force her. You're not going to believe me but I didn't force her. She let herself. I didn't get a good look at her but she's almost my height and she was smelling of custard apple. At first she smelled of custard apple; then she smelled of blood. Look at my fingers. It's as if I had cut myself. That's why I stayed, because she left immediately, she went into the house and I stayed in the patio looking at the dark corridor. I stayed there the whole night looking at the corridor, without knowing what to do. Now I know that I was frightened even before I heard the shots.

«20»

—They were sitting on top of the coach. I approached. One of them lowered his arms. I don't know if he was going to jump. When I raised my rifle, the barrel almost touched his belly. I don't know if he was going to jump but I saw him lower his arms. With the barrel almost touching his belly, I fired. He remained hanging in the air like a kite. Hooked on the tip of my rifle. He suddenly fell. I heard the shot. He got unhooked from the tip of my rifle and fell on my face, on my shoulders, on my boots. And then the smell began. It smelled like shit. And the smell has covered me like a thick, sticky blanket. I've smelled the barrel of my rifle, I've smelled the sleeves and the front of my shirt, I've smelled my pants and my boots: and it's not blood: I'm not covered with blood but with shit.

—It's not your fault, you had to do it.

—No, I didn't have to do it.

—They gave the order to fire.

—Yeah.

—They gave the order to fire and you had to do it.

—I didn't have to kill him, I didn't have to kill a man I didn't know.

—They gave the order, everyone fired, you had to fire too; don't worry so much.

—I could have raised my rifle, only raised my rifle but without firing.

—Yeah, that's true.   « 21 »

—But I didn't.

—Out of habit: they gave the order and you fired. You're not to blame.

—Who is to blame then?

—I don't know: we're used to obeying.

—Someone has to be blamed.

—Someone, no: everyone: everyone is to blame.

—Damn it, damn it.

—Don't worry so much. Do you think she'll remember me?

—In this town, they'll remember us: in this town they'll always remember, we're the ones who'll forget.

—Yeah, that's right: they'll remember.

SISTER

What are you going to do now? You haven't moved. It seems as though you didn't even look at them. But, of course, with what eyes could you look at them. They came near and told you. They told you what we all knew, what we all expected because we knew that it had to happen to her too. What our brother should have known before anyone; now too, because he's the one who's closest to them.   What are you going to do now? No, we already know that you're not going to say anything. You've never spoken when we all hoped you would, when we thought you had to speak, to give an explanation or to request one. But the truth is that actually they haven't said anything either: they haven't approached anyone in particular. The oldest girl, the one who hates you most because she's the one who remembers most, has hardly mentioned it. If you expected her voice to reveal grief or even repentance, she's fooled you once again. She said it with pride, almost with satisfaction. As if she had waited all this time to be sure and now that she is, she's enjoyed throwing it in your face, upsetting your plans for the second time without realizing it.

She said it in the same way her mother said it eighteen years ago, when Father smashed her face with the buckle of the spur that he had just removed. Father had ridden all morning and when we saw him arrive and before he even dismounted we heard him tell you: Go and look for your sister, you didn't ask which one of us because you too knew what it was all about. You knew it in that instant. You walked across the corridor without looking at us and entered the quiet cool of the sewing room where Mother must have been because she immediately appeared and, walking slowly, went to the cupboard, took out a bottle of sour milk, and put it on the end table in front of Father's armchair. She took out a bottle and an embroidered napkin: carefully, deliberately, as though trying to convince herself that her movements served a purpose: that the bottle and the embroidered napkin had a specific function: that the bottle was there to have its lid removed. But suddenly she realized how useless all her precautions were because Father sat down in his armchair and shoved the end table aside and began to take off his spurs. But before Father had shoved the end table aside Mother had already been defeated once again: for although she had noticed it before, a moment before, when she set down the bottle and then the napkin: if she had noticed then that the glass was missing, even at that moment, it would have been too late because Father had already thrown himself off the horse and was heading for the armchair.

So Mother was left standing in the middle of the corridor, without knowing which way to move, hoping that what was going to start would end, without knowing exactly what was going to start and much less how it would end, but knowing that something had to start.

When you walked in front of Mother, with Sister behind you, firm, and almost haughty for the first time, she looked at you and knew. And knowing then, she realized that there was nothing to do, that anything she might try, the most insignificant move, would be useless, would come to naught and that the only thing left to do, just like at the beginning when she still didn't know and when even the glass she had failed to put out seemed important to her, was to wait and then to start thinking again and then, still not understanding, not even the simplest part: the glass: to stop thinking and exhausted by the effort to fall once again into her far-off state: resignation which for her couldn't have the heroic quality of resignation because she never expected anything different.   Father didn't take his eyes off the spur that he held in his hand, the spur from the left boot which was the only one that he had managed to remove, when you and Sister stood in front of him, you a little to the side and she directly in front of him. Father didn't speak. He didn't even ask. There was no need to since he already knew and when he told you to go and look for your sister, he saw that you also knew: not that you had heard

it, or that they had told you, or that they had written it for you
with the dirty, ugly juice of the banana stump on a piece of
sheet, but you knew it and you were sure and that was enough
for him. He didn't lift his head until with a deliberate and firm
motion, he moved you out of the way with one arm, and struck
Sister in the face with the spur. That is to say, with the arch
and the buckle and the straps of the spur because he held it
with his hand clenched over the rowel which dug into his fingers so that when he struck Sister a second time, there was
also Father's blood moistening the dry and now reddened mud   « 27 »
that covered the straps. There was no need for words, but they
were said anyway: not by Father; by her. As if they had been
inside her for a long time, even before this occasion when they
didn't have any company and the words were alone inside her
thin tense body. She said them one by one, calmly, with the
awesome sentence growing as she kept adding words to it. Father raised his arm and the blood drenched his wrist: but his
blood. He didn't hit her again. He stood there with his hand
still clenched over the spur's rowel, but he didn't hit her again.
He pushed the end table even farther away, while the mouth
of the bottle had already become congested with flies, crossed
the corridor and mounted his horse again, still clutching the
spur.　　　　Neither you nor she moved. It was later, much
later, after Mother put the heavy glass on the napkin, that she
went to her room. You didn't do anything to stop her. You
seemed taken aback by her words.

Someone notified Brother, I think it was you. That night
Brother's horse entered the house snorting, almost as far as
the corridor. And there he stayed, all night long, snorting. The
house was quiet and dark. It was hot and humid and the air
smelled of salt and I don't think anyone was sleeping. Each
one of us in our rooms heard Brother's harsh footsteps when
they stopped in front of her bed. Then his harsh voice quietly
filled every room in the house: damned father, damned father.
And that was when for the first time we heard Sister weep.

When the splashing about of the mules filled the air next to
the corrals, you were already up and you must have heard
Brother talk to the stable boys and mount his horse in a hurry:
with the saddle and the reins and the stirrups and the horse
still wet and dripping from the early morning rain. Brother

heard them come in and was waiting for them in the corridor. One of them said: They finally got here. And Brother asked: How many? And the stable boy: They must be about two hundred, two barges came, packed. Then Brother looked at his horse for the first time and said: Let's go, we've got to get there before they do.   That morning, while we were eating breakfast, Carmen arrived with the news that the station was full of soldiers. Sister raised her head: she had a dry glob of blood on her battered cheek. Mother looked at her and covered her mouth with her hands. Then you said: I hope they kill them all. And Sister: they won't kill them all, they won't be able to kill them all. She said it simply, without raising her voice, but with certainty, with absolute certainty.

You were the first to realize that Sister would no longer be the same: Sister had given birth to a voice of blunt and firm words. Above all, firm. If Sister's new voice surprised you a little, you didn't show it. But the fact is that you never let yourself act surprised: you seemed to expect everything: to know everything beforehand. As if everything conformed to a plan that had already been made, laid out, and foreseen down to its smallest details. So that this hasn't surprised you either. And if you now had the eyes to look at her, you would have looked at her the same way you looked at Sister the morning the soldiers came to town: as if relieved: grateful: because what you had expected, what you had foreseen without having a clear notion of it, was taking a definite form and you wouldn't have to wait any more. You already knew what to expect. You could fight against a concrete enemy, a specific enemy; who sat opposite you, with her face battered, her hands abandoned on the table and her whole thin and fragile body defying you with a double and calm defiance.

Carmen added that the station was full of soldiers (full of soldiers from the highlands who had arrived at dawn from Barranquilla and who were going to the Zone to defend the interests of the Company and although they were well armed and many of those who were highlanders said that the bullets were dumdum bullets of the kind that could go through an iron rail, the workers who had gone to the station to see them said that nothing would happen because the strikers were waiting for them in Sevilla to present the list of demands to

the General, because the government had sent them to prevent the Company from continuing to abuse the workers, and
the truth was that the soldiers in the way they talked greatly
resembled the majority of the men that the Company had
brought for the first cutting in La Gabriela, after they laid the
tracks of the branch line and the cars were being loaded right
alongside the banana trees, and they said that the cutters even
had friends among the soldiers because they too were highlanders, but there was one thing and that was that they had
removed the fried-food stands from the station and they had
closed the bar on the other side of the tracks, and they said
that there were orders to keep them closed until the soldiers
left, but they didn't know if the orders had been given by the
Mayor or the General, because the General had not yet arrived
although he was the first to disembark, but a motor car was
already waiting for him and he had left immediately for the
Company offices to talk to the gringos, and since there was an
open track they said he would return at noon, and those who
went to the port say that there are still more coming because
the ones that were coming in the Iris barge were run aground
by the wind in Cuatro Bocas and they're waiting for it to sub-
side, the sailors say that those guys won't have time to go to
the Zone and that they'll leave them here until the others
complete their mission, and they say that the mission is to
shoot, and the "academies" on this side of the line had also
been closed but they don't know why and the "pupils" with
their long dresses are all in the station talking to the sergeants, they say they're sergeants because they're the ones
giving orders to the soldiers and they're not carrying knapsacks, nor are they wearing boots but shoes, and since they're
not dressed in white nor are they carrying swords they've got
to be sergeants, since the girls are from the city and have
been around, they know, no doubt the "academies" will be
opened again tonight). All of us, except you, pretended not to
listen to Carmen. It's true that you didn't ask her any questions, that you didn't interrupt her, but you hung on her every
word and only when she began to speak about the women and
we heard the shrill whistle of a non-scheduled train, a train
that could not be identified because it was unknown, did you
leave your napkin on the table and get up without asking to

« 29 »

be excused.   The sound of the unexpected whistle penetrated our ears and cut off the parade of images that were buzzing around Carmen's tightly packed words. Mother was left with her question dangling from her opaque eyes: a question that nobody, not even you, could have answered for her: because no matter how hard we might think and try to remember the most remote routes, we couldn't have found a time, a place for that train. We lost our points of reference for measuring the time that normally passed between our going to bed and our rising. The regular and perfect routine for every day except Sunday was broken, confused as if someone had methodically messed up a neatly arranged set of dominoes. Only you, and now Sister, knew that that train was the beginning of a schedule, not a new one, strange but not a new one.

Sister didn't need anyone to tell her: little by little she began to discover, to understand, while we were trying to organize in our minds the irregular silence of the trains. I think that she was the first to discover it; much before Father; much before you. And that's why when Father said it, puzzled for the first time in his life: not amazed: puzzled, sternly of course, but with a questioning sternness for the first time in his life, Sister was the only one who didn't look at him. Brother couldn't have told her because he didn't know either. (He didn't discover it, didn't even guess it, while he was waiting for the stable boys to arrive, lying still with the almost dry mud of his boots pressed against the sheets: and his pillows and his nightshirt and even his fingers tinged with the sharp odor of caked blood: lying with his eyes fixed on the roof beams, carefully stretched out beside Sister's open and docile body that suddenly trembled in a dry, stifled sob.) When he heard the horses in the patio he must have thought that he had no choice this time either: he had to leave. But what he certainly didn't think, nor imagine, nor could he know at that time, was that he would not return home. Not because you or Father would prevent him from returning. Or that he himself, of his own will, adhering to what he thought was his duty: to stick by the crushed, stubbornly inserting his life in those who might no longer have the courage, nor the desire, to try again; because it might occur to Brother that it was also his duty to restore in each house, in each corpse what had been removed, the vague and nameless idea that had set them in motion, that had pushed each one of the men and each one of the corpses out of their homes and out of their land which didn't even belong to them, in order to seek the little house, or the little land or the little death that might belong to them: and this, the act of staying among those who had failed, because he was the only one who knew that they had not been defeated: only doubled over on the stations' hot platforms, doubled over by the hot weight of the bullets, but not defeated and he had « *31* » decided not to return: obeying not only this, not only what might or might not be his duty, but the simple memory of the quiet and purposely provoked blood: which could not even be called incest: only his own blood liberated inside a body that could very well be his own: which didn't need to be mixed with his blood because it was his own blood returning. None of this could explain Sister's clairvoyance. But now, after your words, and Father's words, Sister understood exactly because she knew it before everyone: Brother would have no reason to return because she would not be in the house.

If we could understand you better, if some time you had given us the opportunity to know what you were like, if you had even let us enter your room some time, we would pity you now. It would be enough to look at the large empty hollow spaces that have opened up on your face in order to feel pity for you. But you never let us feel that we were your sisters: you never let us belong to you.

Even in the so distant beginning of our memories, you are isolated from us. We grew up apart from you: from your gestures, from your words, from your plainest dresses. You've kept us out of all your experiences, even the most commonplace ones. You systematically isolated us from everything that we might share with you. Yours was yours and from what little we were able to discover for ourselves in our reduced and plain childhood space, you would take what you wanted without giving anything in exchange.   In the early years we followed you around fascinated and frightened, with a fear that you made up and encouraged so that we might not even peek at the magic circus of chicks pierced by the metal ribs of the broken umbrellas and of mice bleeding from where their tails and ears had been cut off that you spun around inside a large cookie box.   Seeing you play with the strangest and most common objects we lost our taste for dolls and ordinary toys. And since we then wanted to be like you, we would imitate everything you did to the point of exasperating you. Then you would be cruel: with a methodical and tremendous cruelty that made us more dependent on your will.   If we had gone to school, maybe we would have had a happy childhood. But when Mother hinted at it, she didn't say it, she didn't even let it be known that she wanted it, that we should be sent to school, Father lowered his newspaper a little so that we could see his eyes and said: What they have to learn they'll learn here. And the next day the daily and boring task of learning the letters, the numbers, and the places began.   You would sit down alone at the center of the table that they placed in the library, and you would follow, silently, all the markings made by the teacher on the piece of black oilcloth that Father had framed on the wall. It didn't surprise anyone that you were the most intelligent of all of us. You were the first to learn to read. Then you stopped paying attention to the lessons, you stopped sitting down at the table, and the teacher stopped asking you questions. You would sit in Father's easy chair, which was too big for you, and you would take any one of the books, which were also all too big for you, from the first shelf, and only when we finished the morning class in order to go to lunch would you put it back in its place. And one day, perhaps when you had finished all the books on the first shelf and when perhaps you were too small to reach the ones on the second shelf, you simply stopped going to class. That afternoon the teacher asked Mother why you hadn't been in class and Mother didn't know what to answer. You had already begun to be a mystery for her, a more impenetrable mystery than Father because you were her daughter, there was part of her in your body, or at least that's what she thought at first. Later, she stopped being concerned: she accepted the fact that in some moment while you were being conceived, while you were developing within the womb, while you were being nursed, a split, a separation had begun. I think that she must have thought that you were estranged from her, and that all

that existed between the two of you was a relationship of sharing living quarters, of sharing a room, and Mother became one
of us; not a separate person with a perfectly defined function
like Father, but one of us. A kind of neutral entity whose existence was tolerated, even favored, but whose voice and whose
actions had no importance whatsoever within that strange
hierarchy which first Father and then you had imposed on
the family.   The fact that you were able to manage
alone, without Mother's help, during all the years of anguish
and of the continual and disturbing discoveries, made us ob-   « 33 »
serve you closely to see if you, if your body, also creaked with
a dull pain like ours.   One day we went looking for
you all morning until we found you in the corral, seated on an
old saddle, with your skirt gathered up above your belly, staring at the persistent trickle of blood that was soaking your
groin. As soon as you realized that we were staring at you, you
moved your legs back together and shouted at us without anger: Go away, go away. That night, Sister, who was still small,
came to my bed and told me: She is like you.

   You're seated on Father's chair, still, as if you were dead.
But you're not defeated. They know it, they knew it from the
time the struggle began: that they would never be able to defeat you: that it would be implacable, constant, never-ending
because you wouldn't let them defeat you. You taught them
to stand up to you, you encouraged their rebelling because
you realized that that was the only way to arrive at an understanding. Not at an agreement or a justification but an understanding. You brought them home to have them stand up to
you: not for them to pardon you but to try to prove to them
that you had been right. But they defined the struggle much
sooner than we all expected. They drew up the rules and an-
ticipated the ending: that is to say that there would be no ending. Many times have we wondered why you keep on. Why you
haven't abandoned everything if you know that a solution will
never be reached, nor will the moment ever be reached when
you and they might say: all right, we haven't even succeeded
in generating real hatred, let's make a truce: not in order to
start again but rather to leave everything the way it is: unfin-
ished.   You've raised them in this house, among us
and our people, imposing them on us, allowing them to eat

our food and breathe our smell, in order to teach them first that they are part of us and then you've patiently waited for them to grow up in order to prove to them that the family will endure, that we shall endure in them, whether they like it or not.   Because that's the only way you have to make Father and his name endure.   Father knew he could count on you to reconstruct and perpetuate what had been broken, undone, ended. That which could not resist when a strong, biting, corrupt, and foreign wind blew— which it didn't resist because it was not built on perfectly established values but rather on weak and tired traditions— it had to be reconstructed. Reconstructed stubbornly on the same worm-eaten foundations that had already given way once, because either it was too late to change them or there were no other ones known or nobody wanted to look for them.   This you understood perfectly, just as you used to understand everything connected with Father. When Father would return home with his pointed beard full of dust and a green stench covering his body you were the only one who would draw near to kiss him without closing your eyes. After the required kiss that would keep burning us all night long, you would stay on his lap until you fell asleep. There was no reason for you to do it because when Father brought presents, they were the same for all of us. We couldn't understand why you liked him.

Once our feelings became defined with regard to the people in the house, once we found out how to distinguish between fear and affection, we chose fear for Father and you chose affection. Even though everything was then perfectly defined, Father continued thinking that it was his duty to treat us all with equal harshness. But you were the only one who dared to break all his rules, to ignore his prohibitions, to dissent from his irrevocable decisions.   We didn't realize when it was that Father decided to accept this fact, he didn't even indicate that he had accepted it. It was a tacit agreement between the two of you, arrived at without saying a word, without establishing conditions. One day you must have looked at each other and at that moment you must have thought: I'm just like him, he won't be able to dominate me, between the two of us we'll run this house, and when he isn't here anymore

I'll run it alone; and he: Here is all my blood, she's like me, she'll take my place, I can trust her. And that was that. There was no need to say anything.   It stayed defined, established. Mother also discovered it without anyone's telling her. She discovered it from one astonishment to the next. And she accepted it as she had to accept everything: because it was a fact. A fact in which she had had no participation at all. Just as, for a start, she had not participated in the selection of a husband. She was simply told: this man will be your fiancé: and then: this man will be your husband. Without explaining   « 35 » to her anything else. Neither what a fiancé was nor how he became converted into a husband. And in the morning, without having been able to sleep, bruised and afraid to look at her moist legs, still puzzled and already without any hope of getting to understand.

Father told you that morning: Come with me. He didn't have to tell you where he was taking you: you knew. You were the only one in the house who knew what was happening. During the four days that the trial lasted you didn't say anything. Not even later. We found out because the town's hatred infiltrated our home like a hot, salty odor. The following Sunday in church, people looked at us as if they were discovering us once again. We didn't know that they had a new reason to hate us.   We found out little by little, as always. Through a dash of the servants' conversation overheard in the kitchen, through an isolated phrase from the seamstress, through a resigned complaint from the men who brought the water jugs at dawn and whom we managed to hear because the heat and our bodies had kept us awake all night long. From the stifled sobbing of the women who began to ask for you we found out about the trial. It seems that at first nobody in the town thought that Father would be capable of doing it. But when they saw you enter with him, they knew that yes he would.

For four days, in the morning and in the afternoon, he faced all of them and accused each one until they were declared guilty. You must have heard awful things because as soon as they realized that they were lost, that an accusation from Father was sufficient, they found the courage to talk against him.   We never asked you about the trial. Perhaps because we knew that it was useless to ask you because you wouldn't say anything, you wouldn't explain anything. You wouldn't explain this new hatred that we had to bear without knowing the reason for it and without being responsible for precipitating it.   We didn't know what was said in the small room of the town hall; the hot and dirty small room, where we later signed the papers for the sale of La Gabriela. We didn't know what Father said nor what you were doing there. But on the fourth day, when you both had returned earlier, we heard Father say: Those were the last ones, we've

wiped them out. And then you: And those who remain, and their children, and the children of their children, will not try to strike again, they will not dare.   And that was it. The trial episode ended right there. We didn't have a right to know anything more. All that was left for us to do then was to wait: to wait for the hatred to pile up around us, to fill up all the necessary time blocks until it exploded, to wait for it to build up to a crisis: to envelop us and dry up the air around us. Around us, not around you. Because you weren't vulnerable to the town's hatred, you weren't vulnerable to what you had initiated: initiated because Father would not have done it alone. The town knew him very well and that's why it didn't expect that he would do it, that he would condemn the leaders one by one with his words. But it didn't count on you. Father needed you, he needed your strength, your contempt, and your desire to perpetuate everything that the name meant. Perpetuate it in any way whatsoever even through hatred. And when the time came for what should have been remorse, it was you and not Father who blocked its way.   The workers' wives, already dressed in their widows' garb, would enter through the corral gate and would ask for you. Not for Mother, but for you. Because the town was already aware of your presence and your strength. It realized that the struggle was against you, that the enemy was you. You would let them speak. Often Sister would hear a few words that reached the sewing room and she'd cry silently. Some of the women would accept the money and would leave in astonishment but those who were beginning to understand their grief would curse you.

What are you going to do with her? Now that she's told you what you should have known, which shouldn't have taken you by surprise because it was the only way she could destroy everything that has taken you so long to reconstruct. What are you going to do now that she has come close to you and with words as sharp and sure as beaks has pecked out your eyes? You don't have time to start over again. To say to yourself: here it began, to remember it, to recognize it and to realize that it's the only starting point for the tremendous task of picking up the pieces of what has been torn down and to put them in their places again. You don't have time because they are not going to give it to you. They are not going to allow you days and months to plan, to search, to solve. They'll insist. They'll hound you until you decide: because their liberation depends on your accepting that they are not part of us, that they don't want to be part of us: that they don't want to be a continuation of something that is finished: of an unoccupied and doomed house. They represent another beginning, a beginning of something that will also be destined to perish like everything pertaining to us: but they want to have the privilege. Especially she who took on the trouble, the pain, and perhaps the disgust of proving to you, in the only way that it could be proven, that you had failed. And the fact is that they don't have time to wait either. And that you also know.

« 37 »

You will not do what Father did: you will not smash her face. Not because they're going to prevent you from punishing her physically but because she'll be totally indifferent to it. And also because you're more intelligent than Father could be. You won't ride three days there and three days back in the same week as Father did, in order to look for someone who might have something of ours and who was at the same time sufficiently different to constitute a kind of punishment, and force him to do something that perhaps he didn't want to do because the small and fortuitous quantity of blood that he shared with us indicated to him that this was not going to be a solution. And then, for three years to effectively destroy everything that the custom and comfort of being together, of eating together, of going to bed together could create. To effectively provoke the moment in which that small and fortuitous quantity of identical blood, now fortified every nine months, three times in twenty-seven months, would rebel in order to ride again for three days and without even getting off the horse, fire as many times as it took in order to justifiably kill the man who from the moment that his birth could not be prevented, not because the attempt hadn't been made, but because that same small and fortuitous quantity of identical blood had deposited him in the unsuspecting womb, the man who must have known that he was condemned to that death alone. And to return to the town with the corpse already bursting and tightly wrapped within the confines of the hammock and to bury him here, so that the town could continue to remember and to hate.

The first sounds of the pounding on the gate must have been lost in the noise of the rain, that's why they couldn't be heard in our rooms. But when the heavy outside gate had been opened for them and they were crossing the brick path between the corrals, not even the rain could muffle the weight of the sixteen hoofs. After the sounds of the boots, the spurs, the machetes, and finally the saddle cushions, the voice, clearly distinguishable from the rain and the tumultuous arrival, filled the air in every space in the house: Not the Mother: notify her.   And then the words: not the rain, nor the tumultuous arrival nor the voice; but the words: They killed him in Sevilla, with the edges of their shovels. And then Mother's unaccustomed weeping.   And the words kept coming: Someone saw him enter Demetrio's house alone and they waited for him in the corral; they swarmed around him like ants pinning his arms so he couldn't draw his revolver, and they must have taken it away from him because we haven't been able to find it. When they released him, the others already had him surrounded with the corpses: they struck him with their iron tools until they knocked him down. When they arrived, he still had the shovels stuck in all parts of his body.   And the words, the weeping, the boots, the spurs, the hoofs, the horses, piled up together in one single sound filling our bodies, filling our bodies, filling our bodies until our eyes burst out crying with hoarse and salty tears.

He went out into the rain and said to you: Come, come and dry off, you're all wet. It was a long time after the soldiers had left. A long time after the house had become filled with the monotonous sound of weeping. He put his hands on your shoulders and pushed you into the dining room. With

your hair stuck to your face and the rain still dripping from
your bathrobe, you looked as if you had just drowned. He put
you in Father's armchair. You stayed there the whole night:
what little was left of the night: still: in silence. You weren't
looking at us. Your eyes, your attention, and your will were
fixed on the rain which separated you from the heavy outside
gate, through which the noise had arrived, the voice and the
words of the first defeat. Sister bent over suddenly, fell on
your knees holding back her dry tears.   Then we
heard your words, but not directed at us nor at anyone, but
rather at yourself and perhaps at dead Father: They will not
see me cry, not me, they will not see me cry, I will not give
them the pleasure.   And the town did not see you
cry.   Although it formed a crowd in front of the
house when they brought the hastily nailed box of damp wood
where Father's pierced body lay. And it waited there the whole
day under the rain, for them to take him towards the church.
And then it waited in the atrium for the priest to throw a little
more water on the box, now better nailed, less coarse, and
even painted black. And it followed it to the cemetery and saw
it descend to the bottom of the hole that had begun to fill up
with the day-long rain, wobbling on the pulley. And it waited
until they covered it with salty mud and placed on the salty
mud the piles of dirty, crushed flowers. And then it crowded
together again in front of the closed house from which the
repetitious and weary music of the rosary chorus barely es-
caped. And, after the ninth night, it no longer returned. Because each one must have thought that even Father's broken
corpse was stronger than the whole town.

   After the ninth day, you still waited for there to be a little
less rain before sending someone to look for them. Not because you had any hope that Brother would return home and
bring them: you knew that Brother wouldn't come, that he
had to be forced to do it and that the only way to force him
was to send for the children: letting him know that you
wanted them in the house: in the house where it was their
right to live and grow up. And you had to give in for the first
time, you had to tell us all: We need to gather our blood, sow
it in the house in order to consolidate what is crumbling
apart.   And this time Brother brought them. And

he turned them over to you for you to raise them and make
them part of the house. And it remained to be seen how they
were to pluck out your eyes and defeat you. Because Brother
knew that all attempts on your part to perpetuate Father
would fail. That's why at this moment he is just looking at
you. Not at them: at you. Waiting for you to accept that
you're both defeated: that Father and you are definitely defeated.   Brother has done nothing but wait. He's
waited for eighteen years and nine months in order to find out
for sure what he always must have felt: that the corpses tossed
along the tracks and piled in heaps on the stations in the
towns didn't mean that he had been mistaken, that he had
been defeated simply because those who had made the peas-
ants bend their bodies over their undrawn machetes were
right. He has needed all this time to see the collapse of the
race from which the rifles derived their support.

« 40 »

You've turned toward Brother. You've turned your round,
hollow, dry sockets to the place where he has begun the mechanical and annoying movement of banging and scattering
the ashes and then squeezing the narrow tobacco leaf into the
pipe. If you had eyes you could see Brother's weariness. A
weariness accumulated in his bones, that has been growing
with him, leading the very goal of his movements astray,
making them less precise, less definitive. A weariness located
within him, not on his skin nor in his muscles but within his
very bone structure. Placed there so that it might not be com-
batted nor expelled. Fixed by the precise idea that everything
that might be done or attempted in order to change what was
determined by Father's will would only lead to losing the opportunity to adjust. A weariness stemming from the certainty
that everything that had been decided for him, even before he
had been born, would endure even after his death: and this in
spite of having at first ignored, then broken, then changed
with his own existence and with the violence of his actions
everything that had been decided for him. A weariness of having to continue struggling against what from the beginning he
knew could not be defeated. Because first he would have to
defeat all his blood and the origin of his hands and his body
within his body itself. And then dissolve all the ties that his
body had created with the people in the house, and this was

not possible.   Because if you could see this weariness now you wouldn't have to start waiting for Brother to
say the words that we all know he's not going to say. That he
won't say them even if he wants to: because he now knows
that once again he will be unable to overcome what is decided
for them: not by Father, nor by you, nor by him, but by their
blood and the house they belong to.   You know this,
we all know it. But you want Brother to be the one who bears
the burden of the words that are going to be said: you want
him to be the one because you don't have the eyes to see his   *« 41 »*
weariness.

It was necessary for them to grow up and pluck out your
eyes. Necessary too for her blood to roll down her thighs voluntarily and for the house to fill up with the damp odor of its
being torn apart. Necessary to break down what you thought
you had reconstructed, only to discover that the blood and the
name will endure, not in the calm but in the wrath and fury
of the blood and the name. Necessary to keep your body closed
and to calm your skin so that nothing might distract you from
your mission of raising them. Necessary for you to laboriously
form within you a fondness for their looks, their voices, their
ways, in order to feel them yours and be able to endure the
long growth period of their childhood without despairing. And
then to overcome the anguish of their sicknesses so that what
might then be love didn't prevent you from being strict for
their own good. Necessary to toughen the natural softness of
your arms to keep from helping them stop their sharp and
lonely crying the nights they were upset. Necessary to foment
hatred against you to make them strong; united; dependent
on you for that very fortifying hatred. Necessary for you to
have overcome your loneliness so as not to allow them to ban-
ish it for you with their triple vitality.

And as though all this stubborn dedication of your limbs
and your guts and your senses to one single purpose: to raise
them: to prepare them so that Father's blood and Father's
name might endure; as though all this had not been enough;
as though sharing this house with them had not been an ex-
hausting job already: you now have to accept what she has in
her womb. Accept it because they didn't give you the chance
to choose: accept it, because if you reject it, her sacrifice will

have been useful and their hatred will finally have defeated you. And the destruction of her waistline will be a small price to pay for their liberation. You told her: He'll be born here and in this house he'll be raised like someone who belongs to this house until someone is born from one of you who can take Father's place.   Even without eyes, you're stronger than they are: stronger than the town, just like dead Father.

FATHER

Father is seated on a rustic chair made of wood and soft raw-
hide. Father is sixty years old and he's strong and tough. When
he stands up, he'll be short, broad-shouldered, with a bull
neck, a powerful chest, a thin waistline, and legs slightly
bowed from having spent the greater part of his sixty years on
a horse. When he speaks, Father's voice will be harsh, authori-
tarian, accustomed to always giving orders. There is no ten-
derness in Father. But neither is there any crudeness. He is
implacable but there is no vengeance or bitterness in him. He
is naturally tough like the guayacan tree.

Father's hands are slender and maybe even fine, but his caresses must be frighteningly painful.

The room where Father is seated is bare and the floor is
paved with cement; the walls are whitewashed and there's not
even a calendar; in one corner, beside the window, there's an
iron washstand with its basin, its pitcher, and its white pewter
pail. The bed is against the other window, beside the only
door, which opens on the yard and not the street even though
it's a corner room. The bed is made of wood, and is wide and
strong; and the thick matting that is placed on the boards is
covered with a very clean sheet. On the bed there's not even
one pillow. In this room nobody lives; it is an unoccupied
room but well taken care of and cleaned every day.

The girl pushes one panel of the double door and they both
open up as if they had been closed under pressure; she enters,
lines them up carefully and closes them with her two hands;
picks up the bolt and places it on its hooks locking the doors.
The girl walks toward Father, who hasn't looked at her yet,
bends down in front of him and begins to unbutton his leggings which continue to stand up at each side of the chair like
two thick dark rolls.

All the girl's movements are mechanical, as though they had been learned a long time ago and practiced very frequently. The girl begins to untie his bootlaces without raising her head.

Father: Where were you?

Girl: In the store.

Father: What did you go for?

Girl: To shop.

Father: Why didn't your mother go?

« 46 »   *Girl*: She's down by the river. We didn't know you were coming today: you hadn't come for many days.

Father: I've told you not to leave the house.

Girl: I don't leave; it's just that I didn't think you were coming today.

The girl stuffs the socks in the boots and places them neatly next to one of the leggings, gets up and stands in front of Father, between Father's bare feet, waiting for the next well-known move. Father loosens the thin strap that holds up his cartridge belt and revolver, a little below the wide belt with a double row of holes for the two-hook buckle that holds up his pants and hands it to the girl. The girl hooks the end of the belt on to the buckle again and places the end on the opening of the cartridge belt and goes to hang the revolver on one of the big nails that are stuck into the door's highest crossbeam.

Girl: I thought you weren't coming today since they sent you a message.

Father: That's why I came: because of the message.

Girl: The message was for you not to come.

Father: That's right.

The girl has turned around and looks at Father for the first time face to face and with her head high. Father is already on his feet and walks toward the bed taking off his heavy khaki shirt.

Girl: I didn't go out to shop.

Father has finished taking off his shirt and the girl moves toward him to take it, turns around and again walks the few steps to the door to hang it up mechanically and carefully. Still with her back to Father who has already started to take off his white-flannel, long-sleeve, round-neck undershirt, the girl repeats:

Girl: I didn't go out to shop.
Father: What for then?
Girl: To listen.

The girl has taken the flannel undershirt and has set it right side out by putting one hand in one sleeve and then the same hand in the other sleeve and has hung it with equal care next to the revolver and the shirt.

Father: To listen to what?
Girl: To what they were saying.
Father: They won't say anything: they're afraid: they're cowards. They'll be cowards for the rest of their lives.   « 47 »

Father is lying on his back on the bed, on the side next to the wall, with his head still and staring vacantly at the intricate framework of poles and vines that holds up the straw roof. Father's hands are resting on his broad chest while his fingers move slowly back and forth over his skin.

Girl: They're not afraid.
Father: They are too afraid: they'll always be afraid.

The girl is seated at the edge of the bed and with the tip of one shoe she takes the shoe off the other foot and then with the toes of her bare foot she takes off the other shoe pushing it off her heel.

Girl: O.K.: they are afraid, but this time they'll do something.
Father: They won't do anything, they won't dare, they're cowards.
Girl: O.K.: they're cowards, but they're going to do something; they're determined to do something.
Father: Why are you so sure?
Girl: I know.
Father: Have they told you something?
Girl: No; they don't tell me anything.
Father: Why not?
Girl: I'm not one of them. Besides it's not a woman's affair.
Father: Whose are you?
Girl: Yours, you bought me.

The girl has taken off her dress and has let it fall in a heap beside the shoes. As she lies down next to Father, with her back to him, with her face turned toward the closed door, her pink percale slip hardly covers her thighs and she tries to pull it down with one hand while she rests her head on the other. The girl's movements now become stiff and awkward out of a strong feeling of shame. She presses her legs together firmly, folds them against her thighs and curls up timidly, not frightened.

Girl: Josefa told me.

Father: What did she tell you?

Girl: That they're going to kill you.

Father, without turning around, raises an arm and puts his hand on the girl's shoulder. The girl stretches, relaxes her legs and keeps lying on her back, almost touching Father, extended as long as Father.

Father takes his hand out from under the weight of the girl's back and puts it on her chest.

The girl closes her eyes.

Father: Who?

Girl: Everyone: the town.

Father: When?

Girl: When you returned here.

Father: Why didn't they kill me when I arrived?

Girl: They'll wait for it to get dark.

Father: They're afraid: they're afraid of me: they won't dare do it.

Girl: They're afraid of you, but now they hate you more.

Father: They've always hated me.

Girl: They always hate those who have money.

Father: No, it's not because of the money: they always hate those who are better than they are. I'm better.

Girl: It's not because of the money, they don't hate you because of the money: it's because of what happened with the strike.

Father: The strike?

Girl: They killed many men in the station: the soldiers fired from the coaches: they didn't get off: the train stopped and the soldiers fired at those who were in the station and then the train pulled out: the soldiers didn't get off but they killed a lot of them.

Father: And a good thing too.

Girl: I didn't see it: I never go to the station, but Josefa told me.

Father: Yeah.

Girl: That's why I told them to send you the message: so that you wouldn't come.

Father: Who told Josefa that they were going to kill me?

Girl: Everyone: the town: they all say they're going to kill you.

Father: But who are they?

Girl: Everyone: the entire town.

Father: It's the same leaders.

Girl: No, those who organized the strike on the plantations were all killed in the station. Not one is left. « 49 »

Father: And a good thing too.

Girl: It's the town: now it's everyone.

Father: No, alone they won't do anything.

Girl: Yes they will: they'll wait for it to get dark.

Father turns toward the girl and covers her with one arm and rests part of his chest on the girl's chest.

Father: We won't wait for it to get dark.

The girl, with her two hands, raises the left side of the slip revealing her whole leg up to her waist and without looking, with nimble and steady fingers starts to untie the knot of the string that holds up her drawers, also made of pink percale.

(1)

—He just arrived; his horse is in the yard.

—How do you know that it's him?

—It's his horse.

—Are you sure?

—Who doesn't know that horse?

—But, did you see him?

—No, I haven't seen him but it's his horse and it has his saddle and the marked stirrups.

—No one else rides that horse.

—No one else.

—And even less so with that equipment.

—That's right, so it's got to be him.

—But they sent him a message: I didn't think he'd come during this whole period of time.

—That's right, they warned him not to come.

—She wasn't expecting him either. She was leaving the store when she saw the horse in the yard: then she started running home.

—It must be him.

—It is him, I tell you it is him.

—Yes it is.

—I didn't think he would dare to come.

—You don't know him.

—And now what are we going to do?

—Now we'll have to kill him.

(2)

—He came alone.

—Yeah, it looks like he came alone.

—It would be better to make sure.

—He could have brought an escort.

—Of farmhands? Why the Gabriela farmhands also left.

—No: the escort are the soldiers.

—Right: the soldiers must be waiting for him at the dam.

—Waiting for him to give them the word, it must be.

—Yeah, waiting for him to tell them to enter the town.

—It would be better to make sure because if he brought soldiers it's better not to do anything.

—No matter what, we're going to do it.

—With the soldiers we can't.

—Yes we can.

—He came alone.

—We don't know.

—Then we've got to go down to the dam to see if the soldiers are there.

—That would be best.

—And what if they're near the railroad tracks?

—No, they're not there; we were on the lookout all morning in the vicinity of the bridge.

—If he brought an escort, they must be at the dam.

—You guys go down to the dam to see; we'll wait here.

—O.K.

—Don't let yourselves be seen.

—O.K.

—And what if there are soldiers?

—It doesn't matter, we're going to do it no matter what.

—Then why did you send them to find out?

—To be sure.

—Are we going to wait for them to return?

—Yeah.

—We have to spread the word.

—Everyone knows already: his horse has been there in the yard for a while now.

—They've all seen it already.

—Yeah, but if he brought the soldiers, you won't do it.

—Yes we will.

—The soldiers have Mausers. We don't have anything: they even confiscated our blunt machetes.

—We have our shovels.

—Our shovels?

—Yeah: our shovels.

(3)

—They're going to kill him; if he stays, they'll kill him.

—Why did he come?

—She sent for him.

—No, they say that she sent him a message not to come: that she warned him that they were going to kill him.

—That's what they say but it's not so: she couldn't stand it and sent for him.

—If they kill him, it will be her fault.

—Right, except that if she sent for him, that alone wouldn't make him come.

—She couldn't stand it, all this time: she's a wild one.

—He's always looked for a woman when he feels like it, not when somebody else feels like it.

—She's a wild one.

—She's just like all of us.

—No she isn't: she sent for him when she knew they were going to kill him. Because she knew that if he came they'd kill him: the whole town knew it. After the massacre in the station they've been waiting for him. A woman must defend her man.

—He's not anyone's man, never was. He doesn't care any more about her than he did about you.

—He always treated me well: I never gave him cause.

—No one ever gave him cause, no one would dare to give him cause.

—He's not bad: he's not as bad as they say.

—He isn't bad: he's the owner: the owner of everything and he can have whatever he wants.

« 52 »   —He couldn't have you.

—Is that what they say?

—Yeah, they say that he's always respected you.

—He didn't want to have me.

(4)

—Now we'll have to kill him.

—Why did he return: could it be that he didn't know?

—He came to force us. He's always forced us to do everything: now he comes to force us to kill him. He comes to arouse our fear.

—No, he came because he didn't believe the message: but when she tells him that it's true, that we're going to kill him; when he becomes convinced that she sent him the message because it's true and for no other reason, that it wasn't one of her tricks, he'll leave.

—He won't leave.

—He'll leave and we won't be able to do anything to him: we won't be able to do anything to him this time either.

—He won't leave because he knows that we're afraid of him.

—Yes, we are afraid of him.

—And that's why we're going to kill him: because we're afraid of him.

—No, that's not why: it's for everything that he has done to us, for everything that he has done to you and what he'll do to me if he continues living: it's for having brought the soldiers to kill us, that's why we have to kill him.

—No, it's out of fear. And also because he's better than we are and he knows it.

—Perhaps he's better than each one of us, but not better than all of us.

—He's better than everyone: that's why we all have to get together to kill him.

—If he doesn't leave now, after having spoken to her, it's because he doesn't think we'll be capable of killing him.

(5)

—We still don't know if we'll be capable.   « 53 »

—There are no soldiers at the dam.

—No trace of them.

—Did you look carefully?

—Yeah.

—There aren't even any traces.

—So much the better.

—Then he came alone.

—Yeah, he came alone.

—It was a lie that she had sent him a message.

—Yeah it was a lie: she's like us.

—That's not what they were saying.

—Yeah, but it was a lie.

—Does everyone know now that there are no soldiers?

—Yeah, as we came back we let everyone know.

—Some of them we'll have to look for in the woods.

—Why?

—With the massacre many fled to the woods and haven't returned.

—The fact is they think the soldiers are going to return.

—The strike ended long ago, why should they return?

—Who knows?

—We can go and look for them.

—Yeah, we can.

—Are there many alerted?

—Yeah, lots.

—Then why go look for the others?

—There's time.

—Is there?

—Yes.

—If you want, let's go.
—O.K., go ahead.
—The horse is still in the yard.
—Now what are we waiting for?
—We're waiting for it to get dark.

(6)

—You know, they're going to kill him today.
—Who?
—Regina's husband.
—The old man who always comes on the pretty horse.
—Yeah, the owner of La Gabriela.
—There's not a horse like it in this whole area.
—Not close.
—He must have others in La Gabriela.
—One of these days let's go there.
—It's very far. And I don't think he has another horse like that one.
—You remember the horses that they brought that time for the fair?
—Yeah, but I like the old man's horse better.
—The spotted one, ridden by the man who had long hair like a woman, was pretty.
—I don't like spotted horses, I prefer the solid-colored ones.
—This year there was no fair.
—I wonder what happened: every year there is one: right?
—Yeah.
—The old man's horse is in Regina's yard.
—Who said so?
—That's what they say.
—Why don't we go see it?
—It'll be dark in a little bit. Darkness carries an evil spell with it.
—And when they kill him, who's going to keep the horse?
—I don't know. Tonight's going to be very dark because there's no moon. If you hear La Llorona, tell me tomorrow, and if I hear her I'll tell you.
—O.K.

—Have you heard her?
—No I haven't. I think the horse is running away.
—He's in the corral.
—If they kill the old man the horse will run away; I know that it'll run away.
—Let's look for a small stone and we'll play hopscotch, all right?
—O.K.
—Or shall we take the kite out?
—No, it's too late. It's almost dark already.

(7)

—It's getting dark now and the horse is still there in the yard: what's he waiting for, why doesn't he leave?
—He's waiting for us.
—For us?
—Yes, for the whole town.
—And what are we waiting for? Why haven't they started to come out of their houses?
—They're waiting for it to get darker.
—Why do we need for it to be dark: we're all in agreement on what has to be done.
—We don't know what we're going to do.
—We need for it to be dark so he can't see us; isn't that it?
—It's not so that he doesn't see us: it's so that we don't see each other ourselves.

(8)

—Did they all return?
—Yeah, they're all in their houses waiting.
—We told them that the soldiers didn't come back and that he was alone in the house.
—They all returned immediately.
—As we passed by we saw the horse.
—It's still there.
—Is it possible that he'll stay the whole night?
—He never stays over: he's never done it.

—It's real dark now.
—Shall we go?
—Let's go.

(9)

—They're coming out of their houses and the horse is still there.
—They're going to kill him.
—Because of that wild gal they're going to kill him.
—No: nobody's to blame for this: not even him.
—If she had wanted to, if she had told him, he would have been able to leave.
—He knew it: he always knew it: he hasn't wanted to leave.
—He's going to wait for them and they won't dare to do anything to him.
—Who knows.
—They won't dare, no one has ever dared.
—Now it's all of them: it's the town.
—They're going to attack him in a gang.
—Yeah: in a gang.
—Let's hope they don't kill him.
—Yeah, let's hope.

(10)

—Let's go home: it's very dark now.
—No.
—It's very dark; what are we going to play?
—Nothing.
—Then let's go home.
—I'm not going home, I'm not going to play anything: I'm going to stay here, I'm going to stay right here all night long because if they kill him, the horse escapes; they won't be able to cope with the horse, no one is going to be able to grab hold of that horse: he's going to escape and he's going to come running past here and I'm going to see him: I'm not going to lose the chance to see him for the last time.

The girl heard the circular and muffled beating of the horse's hoofs in the yard; and then in a quiet rush, in regular progression, the noise of the branches, of the fence poles and the steps on the tramped-down mud, on the thick purslane around the whole house, around the room, around the horse who was kicking and nervously making the harness squeak; the girl heard Father dress quickly but firmly; she heard the metallic noise of Father's belt buckles sliding over the metal eyelets and she heard it fade away as the leather came to rest on leather; she heard Father's boots plant themselves on the room's hard floor; she heard the door being unbolted and the hinges turning noisily. And then all the dull sounds of death and haste stampeded through the defenseless doorway. The girl heard the men charging forward and the struggling; she heard the panting as they surrounded Father; she heard the irregular beating of the shovels on the body that little by little yielded to the unskilled but tenacious attack. The girl heard the thud of the body's fall and the no longer needed thuds of the shovels on dead Father. The girl did not hear words: only the horse's furious neighing and his terrified galloping as he tore through the town opening a wide and everlasting wound.

THE TOWN

The town is bare, hot, and spread out. The first houses start on the far side of the tracks, on the parched dry flats covered with a transparent film of salt. They're wooden houses with rusty, broken roofs through which the rain gets in, and an occasional ray of light when the moon is out. Although the houses are full of women, they are not happy houses: since the women have to dance all night they never have time to decorate the houses nor to plant any flowers. And since they almost never stay long in the town, the houses always seem unoccupied. They arrive at dawn with a small trunk and a paper bag; they hang up their pictures, light a candle, and sit down to wait. Any afternoon at all they gather the things that have been strewn around the room, buy a new bag, and leave: a little more tired, but without knowing it.

The town starts here, here the flats end and here's the Station where the train loaded with bunches of fruit and workers stops. The workers jump off the open cars and the tops of the coaches and the train continues on to the port.

The workers' houses are on this side of the tracks: they're also made of wood and the roofs are also made of sheets of zinc full of holes. But these houses are painted blue and pink and white and in a large corner of the living room encased in a flowered cretonne slipcover and resting on four glass blocks sits the victrola which they play on Sundays and Saturday nights. The men who work on the plantations all week long and who come to town to get drunk and to give part of their wages to their wives and to the other women, began to arrive in groups; or alone; or with their families; some were bringing a dog and a small, pale silent woman. Others only brought a thick blanket rolled up under their arms and a blunt machete.

All silent and strong in their work and silent and persistent in their drinking.

Some stay only a few months: they work, they get paid, and they come to town to sit in the yards of their houses and to look at the mountain peaks. One day they leave without ever having seen the ocean. Others move with their families to the edges of the plantations and little by little form towns along the railroad sidings, on the banks of the fresh streams that come down from the sierra, closer to the mountains.

As the town moves away from the Station toward the center, toward the wide square and the church, the houses and the streets get larger, activity stops, and life becomes more tranquil. Around the church live the plantation owners: three families that have married off their children and their children's children among themselves. And with each death a new hatred springs up and the large plantations become dismembered and the large mansions with their thick masonry walls become more and more inaccessible, more and more isolated. These houses that surround the town square and the church, it seems that they've always been old. On the outside, the salt air destroys them slowly and inexorably, but between the boredom of the women who feel time passing over their unfulfilled bodies and the harsh conformity of the men who once went to Brussels, they provide the force that makes these houses last forever.

The town ends at the seashore: a rough and dirty sea that no one looks at. Nonetheless the town ends at the seashore.

THE DECREE

Magdalena, December 18, 1928

By which the rebels of the Banana Zone are declared a gang of criminals
The Civil and Military Commander of the province of Santa Marta with the legal authority vested in him and

CONSIDERING:

That it is known that the rioting strikers are committing all kinds of abuses; that they have set on fire several buildings belonging to nationals and foreigners, that they have looted, that they have cut telegraph and telephone lines; that they have destroyed railroad tracks, that, armed with deadly weapons, they have attacked peaceful citizens; that they have committed assassinations whose characteristics demonstrate a frightful attitude, very much in keeping with the communist and anarchist doctrines, which the leaders of this movement, which at first was considered a peaceful workers' strike, have spread both by the spoken word in harangues, lectures, and speeches, and in print through the *Diario de Córdoba* and leaflets; that it is the duty of the legitimately constituted authority to provide guarantees to both nationals and foreigners, and reestablish the rule of order by adopting all the measures provided for by civil and military law,

DECREES:

Article 1—The rebels, arsonists, and murderers that now infest the banana zone are declared a gang of criminals;

Article 2—The leaders, agitators, accomplices, and anyone who shields them must be pursued and imprisoned in order to hold them responsible for their deeds.

Article 3—The police are authorized *to shoot to kill* anyone caught in the act of arson, looting, or assault with a deadly weapon and in a word are the ones empowered to carry out this Decree.

The Civil and Military Commander of the province of Santa Marta.

« 66 »

CARLOS CORTÉS VARGAS
General

Major ENRIQUE GARCÍA ISAZA
Secretary

THURSDAY

The woman opened her eyes: she hadn't been asleep: she had squeezed her eyelids shut and remained still feeling how the pools of perspiration below her back and on her stomach were slowly drying up. A hazy light began to filter through the round holes in the roof and the room was readily filled with a chill, dim light. It rained early this morning—she thought—. She looked at the narrow puddle under the door and the barely moist window frame and the patches on the walls that hadn't started to drip yet. But it didn't rain very hard—she thought—it drizzled all night, that's what it was. She closed her eyes and moved about on the bed: she opened her legs, separated them: raised them, moved her arms, rolled her hands over the sections of dry skin speckled with dust and salt. Everything was cool on both sides of her body. She turned around on the bed: on the rough uncovered canvas: she thrashed her legs: she lazily kicked the tangled sheet in which her feet had gotten caught. She brushed her face with her arm and felt her dry lips covered with a sweet crust: she cleaned them with her teeth. She opened her eyes, raised her head, and spit on the floor several times. I wonder if there's any water left in the jar—she thought—I'm thirsty. She let herself slide over to one side of the bed and swinging her legs around looked for the wooden shoes with the soles of her feet: the six slats of the high, rickety bed wobbled and squeaked and the canvas remained taut and smooth for a moment. She looked at the beam in front of her with its one nail resembling a thick, rusty shoot. She looked at the line that crossed the room from one wall to the other: folded over the line, twisted, were the bright green dress and two rags, like diapers, clean and white. She looked at the wall at the end of the line and the four nails wrapped in paper, like fat little fingers in gloves.

The towel—she thought—where did I put the towel. She walked over to the corner where the short-legged table stood with the red clay pitcher, on the soaked plate, also made of red clay. Next to the table, piled up on the floor, the towel, wide, old, with sparse dirty fringes. She bent down and picked up the towel, which was lying in a heap, pressed it against her breasts, her thighs, and her belly: feeling it. She shook the towel and wrapped herself in it, tying it under one armpit. She took the white pewter mug off its nail and inserted it in the wide mouth of the pitcher. The mug scratched the bottom several times looking for water. She took it out half-full and sipped a mouthful. She turned her head and spit it out almost over her shoulder. She tossed the little water left in the mug against the wall and hung it in its place. It tastes like brick— she thought—. Filthy water—she thought—. Wrapped in the towel she climbed back into bed and stretched out face down on the bare canvas. She closed her eyes and thought: Tonight I'm leaving, tonight I'm leaving, tonight I'm leaving. And she fell asleep.

  * * *

  The child ran in under the swinging door and stopped in front of the counter as thought he were lost. He looked at the four empty tables. The mother was seated at the last table, with her back to the entrance. The child went to the table counting his steps and paying close attention to the tips of his white shoes.
  The man put his hand on his head and mussed up his hair. The child shook his head and smiled. The mother drew him to her, almost brusquely, and said to him:
  —What do you want?
  The man spoke without looking at the mother, banging the table with his short, thick glass:
  —Don't you want me to touch him?
  —I'm sorry; it's not that: it's that I don't want to forget him again; he's the only thing I have now.
  —I like to caress him. I always did.
  —I know.

The child moved closer to the mother, backing away from the man's caress. The mother put her hand on his forehead.

—You're hot. Don't go out in the sun any more.

The child began to play with the buttons on the mother's blouse. As if he suddenly remembered, he said:

—Did you hear the little bell?

—No. What little bell?

—You told me that when I heard the little bell, I should come and let you know. You yourself told me to.

The man took a bill from the money that was on the table, next to the already empty glass, and spoke again without looking at the mother, watching the child:

« 71 »

—The little bell on the ice-cream cart.

The mother took the bill away from the child. Now the man looked at the mother; not with anger but with amazement. And he spoke with a harsh voice, as though giving an order.

—Let him have it: let him buy the ice cream.

The child walked around the table on his heels making his fingers walk on the round edge. He made a complete turn around the table and moved his fingers toward the coins that were next to the glass.

—I'd rather have a coin.

—All right.

The man pushed the coins toward the child's fingers. The mother stopped looking in her purse and stared helplessly at the man. The man looked toward the counter and raised the glass showing it to the bartender.

The child stopped again in front of the counter to watch the bartender open a bottle and serve the drink in a fresh glass. Then he ran out into the street banging the door which kept on swinging violently in the air.

The woman said:

—Please don't do it again. Why don't you try to understand?

—Understand what? He'll soon forget me: just as you will.

—I don't want you to do it, that's all there is to it: I don't want you to do it.

—Don't be afraid: everything will turn out all right for you.

—I'm not afraid and everything is not going to turn out all

right for me. How many times are we going to argue over it. I don't want to argue. I can't stand another argument.

—I'm not arguing. What did the doctor tell you?

The woman closed her purse and placed it on the table again. The bartender brought the full glass and picked up the empty one.

The man repeated:

—Did you see the doctor?

—He wasn't in.

And then, in the form of an explanation:

—They put him in jail.

And as if trying to calm the man who had downed his drink and had slammed his glass back on the table:

—It no longer matters.

The man bent his head forward a little and began to slide the moist bottom of the glass over the bare wood of the table. Without looking at the woman he said:

—You won't be able to leave today: the train won't come.

The child came in walking very slowly, holding the cone full of ice cream with his two hands. He passed by the counter and showed it to the bartender; he approached the table and, smiling, showed it to the mother and to the man. Then he sat down with his back to the counter and began to eat the ice cream very carefully.

＊   ＊   ＊

—They'll put a stop to this with bullets: that's the end of it.

—I don't think they'll dare.

—They'll dare all right. They're determined to put an end to this no matter what it takes.

—They'll put more men in jail but I don't think they'll fire their guns.

—They'll fire them; I know them: it's not the first time I'm involved in one of these things: I've got experience.

—Yeah, I know you've got experience but there are so many: so many workers and so many towns.

—That's why the General called for the reinforcements; with the few troops he has here, they can't risk facing the workers. Look: I'm telling you: they're going to put an end to this with bullets.

—If you're so sure, we have to do something to prevent it.

—There's nothing more I can do. I'm leaving tonight.

—You're leaving?

—Yes.

—You can't leave; you can't leave now that the situation is so bad.

—I've finished already: the rest is up to them.

—They don't count any more; now it's up to us to protect   « 73 » the town. They gave the money because they wanted to put an end to the commissaries: you know that perfectly well.

—Yeah, but that's none of my business.

—It sure is our business. We got the town involved in this: all they care about is eliminating the competition from the commissaries.

—No matter what happens, the town will come out gaining something.

—Gaining what: corpses?

—Look, they brought me here to organize a strike, not to protect anyone. As I'm telling you: the bullets will soon be flying and I'm getting out of here tonight.

FRIDAY

The woman woke up: she opened her eyes and heard the noise of rhythmic, pounding steps, more than a noise, a monotonous sound. The woman thought: What can it be. She looked at the darkness of the room and then at the holes in the ceiling and the cracks in the walls through which the daylight would soon begin entering. It hasn't dawned yet—she thought—. The noise, the sound, the rhythmic beat continued filling the room, surrounding it, enveloping it. The woman listened for the rain-drops on the zinc sheets of the roof: She looked at the closed window: she raised her head: she let it fall back bouncing on the bare canvas of the bed: lying still, she looked at the ceiling again beginning to perceive the holes, the crossbeams, the thin rope that held them together. She didn't hear the rain. It's cleared up now—she thought—: and then: It's cold. She turned her body a little to the left, toward the wall and with her right arm she began to pull out the rumpled towel from under her back, from under her bottom, from under her legs. She spread out the towel on top of her chest, on top of her belly, on top of her legs. She raised it a little with her two hands and turned completely over on her left side; she bent her legs, moved her arms together and lay still: her whole body curled up under the towel. What can it be—she thought—. The woman sat up; she lay down on her back again, she pressed the towel with her chin against her chest and spread it out over her whole body; the fringes barely cov-ered her knees. The woman opened her legs and tied the ends of the fringes into little knots; wrapped her legs around the wadded up towel emprisoning it between her thighs. It's the soldiers—she suddenly thought—. She got up immediately and walked to the window tying the towel under one of her armpits; she pushed the shutters in order to unhook the latch, opened the window, and saw the row of men walking on the other side of the tracks toward the station. The woman closed the window and turned back toward the bed: she bent down and picked up her wooden sandals. She sat down on the bed, put on her sandals, and rested quietly with her arms braced on the bedrail, moving only her legs like pendulums. The noise, the rhythmic pounding finally disappeared: the room was almost light, but with a weak light and no glare. She threw herself on her back across the bed: with her shoulders against the other bedrail and her head almost in the air held up by the wall. The soldiers—she thought again—the soldiers. The woman finally got up and began to get dressed.

*　　*　　*

The two men and the two horses were walking resolutely on the soft mud that gave way beneath the weight of the feet and the hoofs. They were advancing slowly and silently, making sure of each step so as not to slip. One of them, the younger, was guiding the horses, by holding tight with one hand to the fistful of reins: almost effortlessly because they were following him docilely, without resisting the short brusque tugs with which the young man was directing them. When they arrived at the railroad tracks they stopped. The horses raised their heads and jerked nervously at their bits. The young man turned around and patted their necks wet from the drizzle: they stood still as though awaiting a new order. The men scraped off the mud that had stuck to the soles of their shoes against the edges of the tracks, entered the roadbed and continued walking unevenly on the cross ties. The horses lowered their heads as if to sniff the rails but the young man extended his arm holding the reins and made them walk beside the tracks. They walked silently for another stretch. And then the young man said: "I came to look for you because they ordered me to." The other man didn't turn his head. "They're waiting for you: two barges full of soldiers." The other man stopped: the horses tried to keep going but the young man separated the reins and with a strong unexpected jerk made one horse cross over to the other side of the tracks: and he asked "When did they arrive?" "A little while ago, they're just disembarking now." The other man took the reins of one horse, pulled down the stirrups that were crossed over the saddle, and mounted with a quick precise motion. He tried to make the horse turn to the right, but the young man had grabbed the reins near the bit and held on firmly. The horse, surprised, moved his head from side to side and pawed the mud with his four hoofs. The young man said: "There's no time now. They're waiting for you." And he let up on the reins. The other man stared at him angrily for a moment while he tried to control the horse and then shouted: "Let go." But the young man had already turned around toward his horse and, mounting, waited for the other man to cross the ties and follow him. Before starting the short, careful trot over the broad muddy flats, he said: "I knew where you were. There's no time for that now either, but there will be when this is all over." "All right, whenever you want," said the other man and the horses began to trot.

« 79 »

*   *   *

The darkness of the room was suddenly pierced by a reddish circle that enveloped the man's face and chest, the woman's back, and a piece of wall with its piece of dirty calendar. The sudden brightness shrank in front of the man's mouth and was eagerly absorbed: then the milky white smoke filled the round hole opened by the flame and the night's darkness was restored inside the room. Then the woman heard the signal: the low, short whistles, like those of a toad, were repeated urgently. The man put on his pants and crossed the room to the door. The woman, by this time awake, sat up in bed holding the sheet over her breasts and with her bare back covering the piece of calendar. The man removed the bar; the rusty hinges squeaked and he stuck out his head and shoulders: then the woman heard the noise of the horses, but she couldn't make out any words. The man closed the door but he didn't put back the bar: he left the smooth guayacan pole in its corner and walked to the trunk, removing his pants in order to start getting dressed. The woman asked: "What is it?" The man replied: "Nothing, nothing."

The woman persisted: "They arrived, didn't they?" The man finished buttoning his shirt and put on his pants. He bent down and looked for his boots under the bed. He sat down again and began to put them on. "What are they going to do?" the woman asked again. The man finally answered: "I don't know." And he stood up. The woman mouthed the words as though they were a refrain that had been memorized by constant repetition: "You don't have to get involved, you're with the railroad, you don't work on the plantations, why do you have to get involved in this." The man opened the door, and before leaving said: "Bar the door." The woman plopped down

on the bed: the sheet slid off her and her large swollen breasts became exposed: The woman tried to pull the sheet up but she only got it as far as halfway up her fat belly, swollen like a big balloon ready to burst. The woman felt it with her open hands and lay quietly: waiting for her eyes to fill with tears and her hands to fill with kicks.

*　　*　　*

One of the men said: "He's taking a long time." "Yeah." And then: "Why did he return, what did he go back there for?" "They told him something about his sister." The man got up. The others continued squatting, sitting, with their arms wrapped around their legs pressing them against their chests; leaning against the crossties; stretched out on the banana leaves—all with their machetes lying at their sides like anchors, looking at the dark, damp opening from which the train would emerge. The man walked to the farthest end of the shed and stopped at the edge of the roof, he looked up as though searching for a break in the early morning thick black darkness that covered everything. He turned his eyes to the men erased by the darkness: barely a few large gray blotches that would suddenly become illuminated behind the momentary glow of a cigarette, revealing a piece of face and the reflection of a staring, expressionless, still eye. He kept on looking, trying to see beyond the boundary of the tightly planted bushes that surrounded the place where they were, and then, like the others, he kept looking at the spot where the train would appear. The man held out his arm and put his left hand under the drizzle: slowly his hand became covered with tiny fresh bubbles that rolled and burst as they came in contact with his finger joints: he held out his other arm, put his hands together and left them there until the sleeves of his twill shirt were soaked.

Then the man rubbed his face and the back of his neck with his wet hands. Later, well after the monotonous drizzle had stopped falling, and when only the heavy drops that had been hanging at the edge of the guttering continued to drip, the man walked the length of the shed again, and moving among the men who were waiting seated, squatting, or stretched out, he reached the place where the horses were tied. "Let's look for them,"—he said—. Five men also jumped on their horses and followed him, crouching low on their horses' necks, as they penetrated the low and narrow trail cleared for the railroad bed.

« 81 »

*　　*　　*

The man who was rinsing the glasses behind the counter put one hand in the basin and felt carefully along the bottom, searching. He pulled out a ball of bluish soap and put it on a board that served as a shelf next to the washstand. He put his hand in again and several times squeezed the piece of rag that was floating on the grayish-brown water in the basin. When it had become a little ball and was almost dry, he put it next to the soap. He turned around and dried his hands on the towel that he had hanging over one shoulder. He looked at the large room, larger now that it was empty, and the big mess of tables and chairs that covered the filthy cement floor. In the back, near the victrola, the man was still there, sitting with his back to the counter, looking at the girl who was talking half-sprawled on the table. He walked to the end of the counter, raised the liftgate to go out but the girl had gotten up already and was coming toward him with two empty bottles in her hands. "He wants another one,"—the girl said—. "I'm going to close now. How long is he going to stay: until dawn again?"— asked the man—. "Why don't you take him to your room?" "He doesn't want to,"—said the girl—"Last night he didn't want to either." "Hell,"—said the man—, and with a sharp jab he uncorked the bottle that he had taken down from the shelf, handed it to the girl, came out from behind the counter and began to close the doors that opened on the small muddy square, at the other end of which could be seen the dark, silent, and almost abandoned-looking station ticket-office with its red and blue mosaic sign. He closed two doors with a tremendous banging of bolts and reinforced them by piling up tables and chairs against the zinc-plated panels. He had already dragged his stool and had leaned it against the frame of the only door that he had left open, blocking the way, and had sat down, and was scraping off the dirt that had stuck all « 82 » day and all night long to the wet wood of his sandals when he heard the splashing of the horses that were crossing the square in the direction of his bar. He must have heard them also because when the horses stopped at the edge of the sidewalk, he had already come out almost knocking her over as he went by. The one who was in front said: "They've just arrived." The bartender couldn't hear what he said, because the latter jumped on the back of the horse of the man who had spoken and the horses crossed the square again and disappeared behind the station. While closing the last door the bartender said to the girl: "We'll have to look for more rum tomorrow." The girl turned around suddenly and said: "There's one left on the table." And she too walked toward the station.

*   *   *

The town began to wake up slowly: it had almost lost the habit of waking up with a start in reaction to the train whistles. The town began to open its eyes and to accustom them to the tenuous darkness of dawn. First it was the amazement at the silence and then the notion, not very clear, that this morning was also out of the ordinary routine maintained for many years, that it was part of a new routine to which the town could not yet have accustomed itself, and therefore, each one's awakening was disturbing.

The town woke up at dawn soaked: covered with an unseasonal and stubborn drizzle that had fallen all night long and was now reviving the forgotten odor of mud that wafted in from the flats. The water had fallen on a parched town full of cracks in the earth that absorbed it through the leaky roofs and the walls made of cracked boards and peeling cement.

The town arose for its morning chores, which would take longer in starting today because the wet wood smoked among the bricks in the stove stubbornly refusing to catch fire. The town went out into its patios: here with the earthy and scalding taste of the coffee, its everyday chores were soon completed. The town stayed indoors, in the patios; idle, without having understood yet but obedient, looking toward the Sierra which with the first light of dawn was beginning to appear, filling up the sky. The town, listening for the signals, waited.

SATURDAY

At 5:10 this morning, at the command post of the troops quar- tered in the Ciénaga barracks, exact information was received about the attack that a group of armed bandits is planning to launch against the railroad station.

At 5:15 the officer on duty orders reveille to be played and the men to form ranks in the central patio where they are to receive their orders.

At 5:30 the desertion of a soldier from the group of reinforcements is reported to the guard office. An investigation is authorized.

At 5:40 the officer on duty orders the cancellation of all passes, even the passes for the purpose of procuring provisions, and a small group of soldiers is sent to look for the orderlies who are on duty outside the barracks.

At the previously cited time, the order is given to relieve the guards, increasing their number to 22. They will patrol the vicinity of the barracks and the church and will be relieved every four hours. The number of the order is recorded.

At 6:00 the men on guard duty raise and salute the flag.

At 6:15, an orderly on patrol duty near the station informed the guard office that a large group of armed bandits has captured a train and that they are preparing to leave for the Zone with the intent to attack the garrisons that have been dispatched to the towns. The orderly is sent with a soldier on guard duty to make his report to battalion headquarters.

At 6:30 the battalion commander orders the reinforcements to leave for the station with strict orders to crush the bandits' uprising. Two hundred and four men leave.

At 6:30 this morning, at the command post of the troops quartered in the Ciénaga barracks, exact information was received about the attack that a group of armed bandits is planning to launch against the Ciénaga station. The troops were immediately put on alert.

At 7:10, an orderly on patrol duty near the station informed the guard office that a large group of armed bandits had captured a convoy and were preparing to leave for the Zone with the intent to attack the garrisons that have been assigned to protect the interests of the Company and of private citizens. The troops, under the command of their officers, moved to the station to restore order. In the face of an imminent attack, the military forces had to fire against the bandits.

Between 9:30 and 10:00 this morning a group of armed bandits tried to attack the railroad ticket office in the town of Guacamayal. The military forces were absolutely compelled to open fire against the bandits. The number of dead has not yet been determined. The wounded have been removed, as prisoners, to the Company hospital. Among the military personnel there are no losses to report.

BROTHER

My sister died this morning. She had to die. It's hard but that's the way it is: she had to die for there to be a little peace in the family. She knew it. It was only a question of time, of waiting for them to grow up a little, of seeing them enough so as not to forget their faces and learn to distinguish them from herself and be able to die without their also dying. But it was also necessary for her to hurry so that they wouldn't get too used to her, so that they wouldn't get to depend on her to such an extent that it would then be impossible for her to die.

She died alone. Detached from everything that might have constituted a pretext to continue living, to continue maintaining a challenge that would have led only to destruction; a challenge that she had not created nor desired but that had been imposed on her, without any alternatives: freed from the task of affirming the uselessness of the challenge with her presence, with her breathing, with the continuing and safe breathing of her three children: unbound, she could die alone.

She must have known that I was returning today, she must have known it with the certainty that she had about everything related to me, a certainty that never needed words, and she must have decided then: now is the time, I've waited long enough, he has returned, now I can also let my body die.

I've returned to her dead body and to her three live children: I've returned to her: I've returned to myself. Once again I'm at the beginning. Then, all the dry and forgotten blood on my sister's cheek, all the dry and forgotten blood on the fingers of a single soldier, all the dry and forgotten blood on the train platforms in the various towns and on the salty mud flats, all the dry and forgotten blood on a dark and narrow street under a horse's hoofs, all this blood for what? Is it going to be necessary perhaps to start all over again?

To start out from the first wound, from the first remorse, from the first shot, from the first revenge in order to come once again, upset and bewildered, to another body voluntarily and calmly killed. I'm tired.

*   *   *

Within this incomprehensible world of relatives and serious faces and harsh words and resigned sobbing that was the big house, my sister and I constituted a world apart. A marvelous and amazing world that we entered each morning with new secrets and new discoveries.

My sister would always be the first to get up. Isabel would drag me almost half asleep and with my eyelashes almost glued shut to the window with the washstand that looks out on the patio with the star apple trees, and when I'd raise my soapy face to catch a breath of air for a moment, since what Isabel wanted was to drown me in the immense washbasin, in the bottom of which I would finally wake up terrified by the monstrous purple butterflies threatening to devour me, the first thing I'd see would be my sister. I'd slip away from Isabel who would follow me to the small patio with the silver jug and the toothbrush, shouting and threatening me with unlikely punishments and we would run to the corral to count how many of the horses had awakened early that morning. Before Isabel could catch us and cram the brush in my mouth, my sister would tell me, with the same anxious voice she had every morning: "Last night I dreamed again. How about you?" And I would answer angrily, lowering my head; "No, I couldn't." My sister would look at me disappointed, almost sad, and would say: "Stupid, stupid." And she would go to the dining room leaving me alone and abandoned, with my shoes that I had just put on already muddy but still wearing my loose madapolam nightshirt since Isabel had not yet finished dressing me.

*   *   *

The big house woke up one morning invaded by a strong, sweet odor. A pungent but pleasant odor that did not belong to the familiar odors of the house and that had surprised me and had not let me fall asleep again after the noise of the milk carts woke me up at dawn. When Isabel entered my room, she was amazed to see me awake and sitting up in bed, concentrating on the odor, excited by its intensity. "What's wrong, you seem dazed." I didn't answer: the odor was mine, I had smelled it first; mine and my sister's. And although I wanted desperately to find out where it came from, I didn't dare ask for fear of revealing my discovery. "Dress me quickly 'cause I'm hungry." Isabel looked at me in disbelief and said: "You « 93 » must be sick." "And you're a witch and you're crazy."

By the time I got to the dining room, the odor had disappeared. My sister had already finished her breakfast and was waiting for me impatiently. "You're always getting up late; the others are going to play in the sewing room, Mother is going to start calling me and we still haven't gone to the corrals." "It wasn't my fault, Isabel caused the delay: I was already awake. I was going to get up right away but Isabel didn't let me." "So, that's what you meant when you said you were hungry. Drink your milk." In one gulp I swallowed the glass of sour milk and went out behind my sister who was walking toward the corrals. I suddenly said to her: "I have an odor." My sister stopped and looked at me without saying anything. I smiled, I loved to have something new for her. "I have an odor that you're not familiar with; let's go to my room and I'll show it to you. It didn't let me sleep. It's not in the rest of the house, only in my room." "An odor of what?" "I don't know; I don't know what, I hadn't smelled it before."

Without talking I crossed the patio and walked toward my room: I knew that my sister was following me silently. When we came out into the hall, I smelled the odor again: sweet, pungent, unknown. "Do you smell it?" I asked without looking at her. I heard her voice behind me, very close; "Yes. What is it?" "I don't know yet but I like it." The odor was in the whole room, mixed with the soapy water and with the towel soaked in the whitish lavender water that Isabel used to scrub me every morning. We stood for a while in the center of the room like two hunting dogs sorting out the odor, associating it with others that we were familiar with, remembering.

—"Let's look for it," my sister suddenly said. "It's coming

from over there, from the direction of the Barracks."

We went through the musty-smelling study, frightened as always; and the room with the wardrobes, dark and damp, that smelled like drawers; and we went out into the narrow alley that separated our house from the wall of the Barracks: and here our odor enveloped us in its strong, overly sweet, overly heavy, nauseating fumes.

We climbed up onto the barricade of piled-up timber that we used to look into the patio of the Barracks, we saw the open shed where they had piled up heaps of large brownish leaves, tied in bundles, and we realized that that's where our odor was coming from. That night my sister, who was the last one to kiss Father before he put us to bed, said to me in a very low voice so that no one could hear: "Father smells the same." I remembered suddenly: I looked at my sister almost furiously, almost tearfully.

When Isabel came to undress me and kneeled down to take off my boots, I said to her furiously and crying: "This room smells like Father, it smells like Father." Without raising her head, she replied; "It's tobacco that it smells of. Now give me your other foot."

*   *   *

I look at the desolation of this house, dead even before death invaded it. I look at the bare, cracked walls, the minimal furnishings barely sufficient for a frugal life without a future; the hard pieces of furniture and the austere beds. Everything is clean and the objects of this house are distributed cheerlessly in an aggressive, bitter orderliness. The house has been sustained by a will to survive and not to last: by a life that knows it has run its course, that knows it is ended, that only waits for the signal during this period of grace granted against its wishes to lie down and die. I look at the substance of this house, already crumbling, falling in bits and pieces, dragged along by the weight of my dead sister's body. I look at all this and I think of the other house, larger, more desolate, and more dead, but based on hatred, fortified by hatred, desperately enduring through the hatred of my other living sister.

What difference will they find? They, the three living children, who will be unable to choose also; as their mother was unable to choose; as I was unable to choose.

*   *   *

I am face to face with a new defeat: the defeat of my sister's body, my sister's life. Defeated by whom? Certainly not by Father because, even before he was crushed by the silent, malicious, calm hatred that he had built up around himself with his vindictive and implacable ways, she had defeated him in the very moment in which he smashed her face with the dirty edge of a spur; not by our older sister who could not help feeling the birth of each one of the children like a frequently repeated death; not by the house, nor by the family that disowned her; not by the new surname imposed on her together with the disgust at the methodical caresses and the sharing of bed and food with a man whose presence at her side was never sufficiently real to affect her: and whose death, encouraged by her, encouraged by the constant fertility of her body, did not modify her fate nor did it free her from what could be considered her punishment: because Father, in murdering the man who three years previously he had chosen vindictively in order to give a different name to what he considered was the disgrace of his daughter, did not accomplish anything except to close the cycle of the planned punishment: the double punishment of delivering her by force and then suddenly depriving her by force; then, who has defeated my sister?

I'm standing in front of her dead body. Her body that I remember as arrogant must now be docile beneath this worn-out, clean chemise that covers it; her hands are ruined, stripped of their skin by the water and the chores for which they weren't made; her hair is still long and black, but the scar on her cheek is now less vivid.

I now touch the scar just as I touched the still moist wound that night and I think; here is where the defeat began: I'm the guilty one, it's not Father, I'm to blame.

*   *   *

I would always arrive late at the small table in the dining room. In the morning it was Isabel who was to blame. We could never agree on what clothes I should put on. She followed a strange rule of choosing my clothes according to the weather, according to the heat, the wind, and the rain. On the other hand, I thought that I should dress according to the games I had planned for the day. If I woke up one morning with the desire to go to the corrals, and that invariably occurred every morning, I would ask Isabel to put on my boots. I would pose the question in a neutral, almost indifferent tone: "Are you going to put on my boots today?" Isabel wouldn't answer. She would open and close drawers, prepare for the disastrous first battle around the washstand, pick up everything that had been left scattered on the floor, and would put it once again in its place, without acknowledging my question. Anticipating her intentions, I would say to her almost shouting: "Isabel, today I'm putting on my boots." When she'd turn around to me, she'd already have in her hands the despised red and white shoes with which I couldn't go to the corrals because if Father saw them on me dirty with mud at lunchtime, he would punish me severely. Without saying a word for fear that the furious crying that filled my eyes and throat would burst forth, I would begin the silent resistance by stubbornly bending my toes. Isabel would enjoy herself trying to straighten out my toes and put them into the shoes. After a few minutes of this game, I'd forget my anger, and since Isabel would tickle the soles of my feet, both of us would laugh and I'd let her put the shoes on without protesting.

When I'd get to the dining room, there was no longer anyone at our table. My sister would wait for me seated in the highchair where they used to feed me when I was little, and from there she would watch me partially eat my breakfast in silence. When Isabel would return to clean the table where we ate, my sister would get down from the highchair and would go to the clean paved patio where the gigantic star apple trees covered almost the whole sky. I would follow her. My sister would say to me: "It rained at dawn, let's go pick out the crickets from among the begonias. When it rains, the begonias are always full of crickets in the early morning." Then she would look at my shoes. "Never mind. Instead we'll go to the study and I'll tell you what I dreamed last night." I would then become happy, incredibly happy, that I hadn't been made to wear my boots.

*   *   *

Standing before my dead sister, I have no tears, only questions. We were deprived of crying after infancy: the hatred that we didn't understand and on which the continuity of the family was founded dried up our tears, denied us the solace provided by crying. All that I have left now are questions; the questions that I couldn't ask when it was necessary to ask them, when they would spring forth, tormenting me at the time of each event, each act and tormenting me even more and oppressing me after each catastrophe. The questions that I didn't have time to ask because everything suddenly fell on top of me with the violence of the unexpected and inescapable wind that blows down the banana groves, destroying what had been security and hope. First Father, who burst into my life like an implacable evil force, suddenly destroying the delicate order of adolescence, the marvelous and promising continuation of a childhood protected from all outside surprise; Father for whom questions were an insult to his irrevocable all-powerful decisions, established by his mere existence the impossibility of asking questions.

Then the lonely hallucination-filled years at the far-off school which didn't allow the questions because the answers were beginning to appear terrifyingly clear; still inadmissible within the entangled state of my confused feelings. And then it was necessary to exhaust my senses, bury myself under a heap of sensations, cover my skin with my hands, against my own wishes, in order to keep out the questions that prowled around me like hungry, ferocious animals. It was the long night of dreadful perceptions. And its memory is only a faded mass of faces, words, sensations without any explanation or consequence.

And finally, all the questions that couldn't be asked when the workers' few miserable years of life were ripped away from them with bullets in the stations all along the railroad line, in front of the half-open doors of their homes, because they were precisely trying to exercise what they thought, and basically what I thought, was their right to ask, to inquire about the reason for the inequality and injustice. The questions that then had to be postponed because it was more urgent to reconstruct what a despicable military man had tried to destroy; to stop the flow of blood that he had turned on. All questions were now piling up in the face of my sister's death. Where shall I find the answers? Could they be within me? Or is their painful and now definitive and total answer in the dead body of my sister?

I used to hate the rain. I feared it more than the worst punishment because rain kept me away from all the pleasant things that the big house offered my childhood with its labyrinthine world of corridors, rooms, patios, and enchanted places that my sister and I eagerly explored every day. The rain was always preceded by an infernal heat that not even the high, thick walls of the big house were capable of keeping out; it infiltrated the rooms, it invaded everything, it dumped itself heavily on the house's objects and people. All of a sudden, the sky would surprisingly turn gray, the clouds would pile up on the mountain peaks covering them with a dirty and frightening nimbus; and a sharp, icy wind would pass minutely over our bodies.

The deafening thunderclaps would relentlessly bounce off the walls of the huge gray bell with which they had covered our patios. Finally, through the luminous cracks opened in the sky by the thunderbolts, the first large drops would come pouring like lead, which on crashing against the bone-dry dirt would raise a minute cloud of dust. Then, in the midst of the din caused by the rain, you would hear Isabel's worried voice as she searched the whole house for me shouting: "This cold wind is going to harm you! Don't get wet in the rain because you'll get sick!" In those moments, I used to hate her. My sister and I would hide pressed against the archway of a corridor, or underneath the ledge of a closed window, or precariously protected by the leaves of the low bushes in the patio with the star apple trees. By the time that Isabel would find us, the rain had already soaked our clothing and a gentle and pleasant coolness was beginning to cover our wet skins.

And at dawn of the following day when the growing congestion in my chest, which I had tried to hide during dinner before my sister's knowing eyes, would choke me and prevent me from breathing, I would have to call Isabel. Seated at my side, scolding me in a low voice, but affectionately, and rubbing my back with her large, soothing hands, Isabel and I would watch the morning penetrate the cracks of the closed windows. My sister would silently half-open the door to my room and would stand there looking at me. When Isabel would leave to let everyone know that I had woken up sick, my sister would come up to the bed, touch my burning head with her cool hands, and say: "I couldn't sleep last night either: I was choking." Then she would leave. And the days of being cooped up in my room with the illness that would begin at that moment would seem more bearable.

*   *   *

Where is my place now? What is my spot in this great chaos of life? Sister has occupied with her body the only place that belonged to me: it was a single death for the two of us and she has hoarded it completely for herself.

*   *   *

The suit was new; the shoes were new; the shirt was new; the tie, out-of-date and too tight due to Isabel's inexperience, made me move with difficulty and clumsily in the heavy traveling clothes that I was wearing that morning.

Twenty days earlier Father had said as he sat down to dinner: "There's now an opening for you in the school." And immediately, without waiting for Mother to finish saying: "But he's still very young; he's barely twelve years old": as if he hadn't heard her: "He'll go on the boat with the next banana shipment. We'll have to get him ready." Mother repeated; "He's barely twelve years old," but now without conviction, without strength, by this time almost with tears. I looked at my sister. It was not the surprise that choked my eyes and throat: we had expected it: we knew it was coming: we knew that one day Father would say these words. It was the shame of having suddenly grown up.

That night when Isabel entered my room with the glass of warm milk that she always made me drink before going to bed, I had already taken off my clothes. Isabel put the glass on the night table where the medicine was kept, covered it carefully with the plate and looked at the things I had strewn on the floor but she didn't pick them up; she came to the bed and sat down at my side saying; "You must be happy, you'll no longer have to wear clothes sewn by women: women don't know how to make long pants . . ." She tried to continue talking but instead of words, large, thick, and abundant tears came out of her, tears that she tried to brush away with the still smooth back of her hand. I hugged Isabel and nestled my head close to her clothing which always smelled of cananga and finally I was able to cry softly until I fell asleep in Isabel's lap.

The days rushed by one after the other. The surprise at the new things that were gradually filling up the huge trunk that Father had brought from Santa Marta and the pleasant sensation of seeing myself converted into the center of attraction for the big house had me dizzy, removed from the routine of a childhood that was beginning to move painfully into the distance, because when I would interpret Isabel's long periods of silence as a feeling of abandonment at my departure and when I would seek my sister's encouraging look, she would lower her eyes and pretend to be thinking of something else. I would become furious and I'd go out to the corral with my new shoes or my new clothes that they were trying on me without caring whether the piled-up wet yellow grass would get me dirty. When my sister would find me, she'd come close and squeezing my hand with her two hands, she'd say to me: "I cry more than Isabel; and more than you."

On the morning of the trip, after kissing the whole family for the first time, I had to go to Isabel's room because as soon as she finished dressing me, she had locked herself in and didn't want to come out. On the way back to the living room, I found my sister waiting for me at the entrance to the dining room. "Return with those same starving eyes: that's all that I want." I was going to ask what was that, but the train's impatient whistle stopped my words and now all I could hear was Father's harsh voice calling me from the door.

THE CHILDREN

—Now she's going to say that she knew we'd pluck her eyes out.

—No: I hope she doesn't start.

—Yes, she's going to start and she won't stop until she gets to cry.

—Cry, no; it'll seem ridiculous for those two large cavities to produce only small teardrops: she'll say that she knew we would pluck out her eyes but she won't cry.

—I wish she would cry; I wish she would cry.

—Keep quiet.

—Everything upsets you now.

—It's not my fault.

—You don't mean to tell me that it's mine; you don't mean to tell me that I was the one who frolicked.

—Leave her alone: we said that we wouldn't talk about that any more: we said it was done and there was nothing we could do about it: the three of us have accepted it: we agreed: why do you insist on talking about it?

—I'm not insisting; it's Sister who's starting; I wish it weren't even mentioned.

—But that's absurd: the three of us accepted it; we're in agreement.

—I accepted it; but I'm not in agreement; that's different.

—And when it's visible: what are you going to do when it becomes visible?

—I can see it already; I've seen it from the first day and I'm bothered by the way Sister carries it; almost with pride.

—I too would be proud; I'd put on a long white madapolam nightgown and I'd walk barefoot throught the whole town with my hands on my belly.

—You're crazy.

—Crazy, no: happy: for the first time, happy.

—If once we were happy, I don't remember it anymore and now I know that we'll never be happy again.

—No: now we'll be happy because we have peace.

—Peace? Look at Sister; you think that we can have peace while that blob of strange,—filthy—, blood chokes her from within.

—Shut up. Shut up. Isn't it enough? We've plucked out her eyes. When is it going to be enough?

—It's never going to be enough; not even death will be enough; it wasn't for Father; nor was it for mother.

—We're different.

—Different from whom?

—From Mother.

—We're just like Mother.

—No we're not: we're stronger: there are three of us.

—Mother was strong. She wasn't defeated. Every day of her life was a protest and every day of her death is a victory. We're the defeated ones.

—What was Mother like? Do you remember her well? Do you remember when we lived in the little house near the sea? I hardly remember.

—Mother was sad.

—I remember the mango tree in the center of the patio and how cool the earth was around the pool: and I remember your kites.

—Mother used to cry at night.

—I didn't have kites when we lived with Mother.

—You didn't have kites?

—No; we didn't have toys.

—Mother did nothing but look at us. She watched us grow. And each year she was sadder.

—I don't remember birthdays in the house by the sea: I don't think we had birthdays then.

—My first kites were made for me in this house; Brother came in one day with a pile of colored paper and a piece of bamboo; he taught me how to make them and then we would fly them from the roof; he didn't have to teach me how to fly them; that I knew by myself.

—One day he died.

—Do you think Mother loved us?

—I don't know. She didn't have much time to get used to us.

—She must have loved you: she did have time to love you.

—Mother wasn't allowed to be selective in her affection.

—I'd like to be able to remember Mother; I'd like to be able to say: she resembled you: or me: but I don't know what her face was like: or whether she was tall or short like me: I have no trouble in remembering places in the house but I can't picture Mother.

—Perhaps it's better that way; it's less sad.

—Why: I'd gladly remember Mother. « 105 »

—Mother was never happy.

—This house has never been happy.

—One day it was happy: the day that Brother made you the whistle with a papaya shoot and you blew it until your lips were swollen: we girls marched after you through the whole house: I always remember that day.

—But by the next morning the whistle had become wrinkled; withered; I cried when I saw it; that's the way everything is in this house.

—Now everything will change; at least for us it will change.

—What will change?

—Everything will change; we're no longer part of the hatred; we're no longer condemned to hate; we're no longer the continuity of this house: Sister has freed us.

—Sister has tied us to another hatred; to a new hatred that we didn't know: that we still don't know but that we have to create within ourselves; our hatred.

—Why are you blaming Sister? Are we going to spend the rest of our lives blaming each other: are we going to recreate in ourselves the lives of the people who constructed this house: this town: this race: the lives that were destroyed just as these walls were destroyed because they clung to hatred? Then what purpose has everything served? Why Mother's protest: why Brother's hope?

—I'm not blaming Sister; I'm not blaming anyone; I'm saying that we've replaced one hatred with another; that we haven't freed ourselves from hatred: that this house and those of us who carry the blood of this house will never be free from hatred.

—Yes we will free ourselves: because each time we belong

less to this house and because each new blood is more distant from Father's blood.

—It's no longer Father; we didn't even know him.

—But its Father's blood that drew us to this house: it's the cause of our birth.

—It's her insistence on keeping his memory alive. Although she hated mother because she was the first to defeat the hatred by defying Father, she has brought us up to be part of this house, of this blood, and of this hatred.

—Yes: and if we succumb to the hatred, she will have triumphed.

—We've already succumbed; she's pushed us into it; she's pushed Sister into hatred.

—No. There's no hatred in me. Not even disgust. It's only weariness.

—We were brought here and raised with a purpose and that purpose has been realized; we're part of this house as much as Brother, who also rebelled and who was also defeated; nobody has won; she has been defeated, but in order to accomplish it, we too had to be defeated.

—No: we've won the freedom of choice; we've imposed our freedom to decide our own lives: just like Brother.

—Brother didn't decide anything, nor shall we; when he returned from Brussels and joined the strikers he did it out of hatred for Father, not out of conviction.

—It doesn't matter why he did it: the reason doesn't matter nor does the fact that they were dispersed by bullets.

—And when he returned after the persecution and after Father's death and after all the other deaths he did it out of love for mother; out of love for us; but he brought us to this house driven by hatred.

—He brought us to prove that he had been right: to prove with our mere existence that in spite of everything mother had triumphed: that he had triumphed.

—Brother has survived; not triumphed; and if he brought us, it was to continue the fight.

—Brother loves us. He's the only one who has watched us grow with love. Whatever little happiness we've had, he has given it to us.

—And to you: more than to us: he has devoted his time and his affection to you: you two are friends.

—The first nice thing I remember is Brother's presence; the almost clumsy way he has of being affectionate.

—His presence: he's the only person who is close to us and we know nothing about him: we've thought about him during the moments of petty despair of our childhood and we've been growing up near him as if that's what was expected of us: but nothing more: what ties us to Brother is an unnamed relationship that goes far beyond the simple family and home relationship. « *107* »

—And to her; what ties us to her; what has tied us all these years?

—To her we are tied by hatred.

—But she doesn't hate us: I'm sure of that.

—It's not a hatred of our names or of our bodies. It's a hatred of everything that signifies a change or a contradiction of what she thought was constant and everlasting.

—But we hate her; we hate her with a hatred that she herself has placed within us.

—I don't know. I couldn't say that I hate her and be absolutely sure. I remember the devotion and energy she invested in us and I can't conceive of there not being any affection in any of her actions. Her zeal to make us better cannot be totally without love.

—I've heard her spend entire nights at your bedside without sleeping: watching over your illness.

—I've woken up choking in the middle of the night and I've seen her enter my room terribly distressed; but that was in our childhood.

—Our childhood has just barely ended.

—In this house we age suddenly. Not like in normal homes where people age slowly and gently. One day without any sign. Without it's being a special or expected day. Any day at all time attacks us, striking our bodies, shrinking us and making us old.

—That's why our childhood seems so distant to us now.

—Here time doesn't flow calmly and gently toward death: it invades us: it invades this house and these corridors and these rooms like a flood: and it drags us away and destroys us.

—Today has been one of those days.

—Time has caught up with her and has destroyed her and has cast her on the chair where Father used to sit. I had never seen her so old.

—It's not time that destroys in this house; it's hatred; the hatred that supports the walls eaten away by the salt air and the rotted beams, and that suddenly falls on the people overwhelming them.

—And suppose it wasn't hatred: suppose it was raising us that has aged her: suppose it was the effort of having raised us alone and against everyone with the exception of Brother: even against the memory of Father who would definitely not have accepted us in this house: suppose it was having to carry the whole weight of the house on her narrow shoulders: a house that if it had not been for us, it would not have been necessary to maintain: because without us it would have come to an end naturally: but because of our existence it had to be maintained.

—For eighteen years she has painfully maintained this house with only one purpose.

—Us.

—Yes; but in order to perpetuate Father's name.

—It doesn't matter: we're alive and Father is dead: we are the result.

—If that's right, we will have doubly defeated her. Defeated her in what she wanted to have endure and defeated her in what she might have learned to love.

—I don't think she has ever loved us; I don't think she loves us now.

—In my present situation, she couldn't love me any more.

—You too want to convert it into guilt?

—No, into guilt, no. But not into sacrifice either.

—No one has talked about sacrifice: no one has labeled it: it's a fact: that's all: it's sufficient to free us: the struggle is finally resolved: ended.

—There's more than that; I think that there's much more; we have been raised as instruments but we're alive; we're human; hatred has not dried out our skins. My skin has not been the cause. This I can tell you.

—Nor has it been planned; it's not the result of a calculated and carried-out revenge.

—No: it's a fact: nor is it a pretext either.

—Nor is it a justification.

—That least of all.

—Then; then what is it?

—Do we have to talk about this again?

—Yes.

—We're not passing judgment on Sister; we're accepting her: as we accept ourselves: we're not three people: we're only one. « 109 »

—I ought to have an explanation. But I don't.

—It's not necessary to explain anything.

—I'm not asking for explanations; but I want to be sure that it's just.

—I couldn't tell you if it's just or not: it was inevitable: that I do know: that it was inevitable.

—The fact is that if we don't talk now, we'll be full of hatred and then we too will be defeated.

—We're defeated no matter what.

—Yes: no matter what.